to

H

for putting up with it all

# WESTSIDERS

OF THE TOWN OF CORNER BROOK, NEWFOUNDLAND, CANADA

## by Tom Finn

"Well-crafted ... character-driven.  An impressive book of short stories about people going about their lives, experiencing change, facing hardships.  Finn writes skillfully and his style is particularly suited to the short story."

- Keith Collier, reviewer
Newfoundland Quarterly, Spring 2011

"Tom Finn's stories demonstrate consistently controlled use of language, and the author's sense of dialogue is keen. It is tuned to the way people speak, and the way his characters speak and think. At times comic, it harmonizes well with Finn's often wry, omniscient third-person narration. Finn writes well, and these stories are good ... some real gems."

- Darrell Squires,
Library Resources Board, Newfoundland, 2010

**Princes** (short stories)
"... Finn has done for pre-Confederation Newfoundland what James Joyce in his stories did for his native Dublin."

- Daniel Jones,
Books In Canada, 1991

## PB

Westsiders
© Tom Finn 2010

Petra Books.
Ottawa Ontario Canada
613-294-2205 | petra@ncf.ca
petrabooks.ncf.ca
Design, editing: Peter Geldart
Consulting editors: Danielle Michaud-Aubrey
Penelope Sparling
Fonts: Arial, Garamond

Cataloguing in Publication
Library and Archives Canada
Finn, Tom, 1931-
Westsiders : old Corner Brook / Tom Finn.
1. Corner Brook (N.L.)--Fiction. I. Title.
PS8561.I554W48 2010  C813'.54
C2010-901933-4


In this fictional work any resemblance to persons or entities past or present is coincidental.

Cover illustrations: Broadway, main street, Corner Brook West, 1940s. Sketches by Tom Finn, 2010

*When In April* was first submitted to The Dalhousie Review in 2011. dalhousiereview.dal.ca

ISBN 978-0-9868263-3-7

*Also by Tom Finn:*

*Malpeque Bay: A State Of Mind*

*Princes*

# CONTENTS

# SHORT'S LONG DAY

W hat a night, wha`t a night!" Sergeant Harry Burns of The Royal Newfoundland Constabulary, amateur thespian and raconteur, cleared his windpipe theatrically, gave his audience a long heavy wink of the right eyelid, and began to read from the night-shift occurrence book, over which he first made a small sign of the cross and then raised mockingly to his lips. Sergeant Cyril Short and Constable Art Bugden exchanged resigned glances and sipped at their cups of boiled black tea.

"10:45 pm. Break-in reported at 18 Howley Road, West Side, the residence of Jilly Evans, poor old Freddy's widow. The second one she's had, by the way, or the third. Break-ins I mean. Seems Jilly, when it happened, was at the Masonic Hall for the regular Thursday night soirée, escorted thereto and therefrom by Mister Tommy Mugford, next door neighbour and widower. That is to say, the break-in must have occurred sometime between about 7:30 pm and the time they got back after ten o'clock. Constable Humby, by the way, attended."

"Anything taken?" asked Short.

"Oh yes, indeed there was, indeed there was, Sergeant Short. It seems a roasted chicken, freshly done and left to cool, was snitched right out of Jilly's oven, with some minor damage done to the range in the process. Fresh-roasted chicken taken, gentlemen. A fowl deed, you might say."

Short and Bugden acknowledged the pun with sour grimaces. "Was that it? Just the chicken?" asked Short.

"The chicken and ..." Burns held up a beefy

forefinger and paused for effect, " … and a 40-ouncer of gin. Beefeater, unopened, and purchased just that very afternoon by the victim herself. And not only the gin, mind you, but also three crystal tumblers, blue in colour, part of wedding gift from Jilly's dearly departed mother. Irreplaceable they are too, according to Jilly, great sentimental value and so on."

"Chicken in the oven, eh?" mused Constable Bugden. "Well, that's more than old Freddy ever got in there, right?"

Clumsy that was, and in bad taste too, thought Short, who did not much approve of the constable's remarks at the best of times. Sergeant Burns, however, smirked appreciatively.

"Now then, 9:50 pm," Burns resumed his reading, pausing to refresh his vocal chords with a swallow of milky Orange Pekoe. "I'm taking things in reverse order here, as you can tell, and let me see now. Oh yes, 9.53 to be exact. Phone call from Lark Harbour, the Reverend Thomas Dinney on the line, Thundering Thomas himself. Seems a Mister George Murrin has gone and got himself shot in the upper arm, left hand side, by an assailant armed with a .22 caliber rifle which the Reverend Tommy now has in his possession. A Davenport Brownie, by the way, in case you're interested."

"Were you able to get hold of Bill French, Harry?"

"As a matter of fact, Sergeant Short, believe it or not, I got hold of Billy on the very first try and the Lone Ranger …"

"Hi-Ho Silver!" predictably, from Bugden.

" … should be there by now. The missus wasn't too happy though, I can tell you. Seems they're supposed to be off camping today and his relief didn't turn up as scheduled. Oh well, a policeman's lot, eh?"

And his wife's, Short thought sympathetically, if she was foolish enough to marry him. "I presume Tommy knows who did the shooting?"

"Of course. The whole parish knows it and even witnessed it, come to that. Able Seaman Felix Andrew Moss it was, Royal Canadian Navy, home on an overnight pass from *HMCS Caledonia*, which vessel, as I'm sure you know, is anchored right out in the Humber Arm at this very minute."

"Not Micky Moss, by God!" exclaimed the constable, his teacup rattling in its saucer. "Sure I went to school with Micky — Felix, but we used to call him Micky — when he lived over on the West Side. Well, by the Lord!"

"Is that so?" said Burns with a raised eyebrow, and then continued his account of the out-the-bay incident. "Seems the regular weekly card game was in full swing in the church basement, the Good Shepherd Guild in charge as usual, when in comes the AB Moss aforesaid, rifle in hand, or arm in hand you might say, takes aim at a certain Missus Minnie Moss, fires, and I'm happy to say, misses the missus by a cat's whisker. As you've probably guessed by now, Missus Minnie is the missus of the shooter AB Moss." He paused, regarding Short with a sly grin. "I wonder, Cyril, if those auction games aren't getting a bit out of hand, d'you think?" But Short, a United Church man, as Burns well knew, only smiled tolerantly at the gibe.

Constable Bugden downed the last of his brew and thumbed pursed lips. "Now that's really queer, Sergeant. Tell me, was there only the one shot fired? Because my old pal Micky wouldn't miss a fly at a hundred yards unless he wanted to. I remember from the old Armory days, y'know, best shot in the corps

Mickey Moss was. Absolutely deadly."

"Well, keep in mind now that the Reverend was more than a little agitated, plus there was the usual static on the Lark Harbour line, but yes, according to my notes here, there were in fact two discharges from the weapon in question. Number One, as I have it here, missed Missus Minnie by a quarter inch; she felt the breeze of it going by her left ear, she told Tommy — went through a basement window and no doubt ended up out in the bay somewhere. Shot 'two', following right after shot 'one', grazed the unfortunate Murrin, as already related, in the upper part of his left arm, went slightly astray thereafter and embedded itself in a corner of the Union Jack hanging on the basement wall. So, a near miss and a nick and, whether through plain luck or, as you suggest, Constable, through deliberate design, no serious harm was done. Thanks be to God. And thanks be to God, too, that it's Billy will have to deal with the Canucks."

"While the cat's away … ?" wondered Short, regretting immediately having given in to temptation.

"Minnie Moss will play," finished Bugden, and even Short had to join in the laughter.

"Yes," sighed Burns in mock dismay, "another war casualty, I'm afraid. But now, gentlemen, on to the evening's highlight. Twenty-eight past nine it was — Constable Organ, God help him, reporting. Brawl over at the Caribou Tavern, US Air Force personnel versus some local heroes, again with no serious injuries noted, at least nothing life-threatening. MPs were Johnny-on-the-spot and picked up AF people Ripkin, Berriman and Caldwell, all ranked as corporals …"

"Soon to be PFCs again," put in Bugden.

"…one, by the way, with a possible broken nose,

Berriman, Garfield, USAF 2765438, to be specific."

"Off-limits, The Caribou," observed Short, and in unison with the others shrugged resignedly. There were times when they wished the whole island was off-limits.

"One of our local heroes is presently at the hospital as a result of the to-do, fractured jawbone suspected. And that's Mister Gerry Tucker, no less, who appears to have finally met his match."

"Too bad it wasn't his bloody neck," Bugden said fervently. "Serve him bloody well right as far as I'm concerned."

And therein lies a tale or two, thought Short. "Who did the job on Tucker? Must have been some punch to crack that jaw."

"Not known for certain, Sergeant, everything topsy-turvy as you can imagine. Constable Organ thinks our Yankee friend with the sore nose, Berriman, hauled off and clobbered Gerry with a bottle of booze, half-full or half-empty as the case may be; but it's also possible, so he reports, that it was actually Ripkin, Charles USAF 288 etc … or even Caldwell, James, USAF whatever, who up and actually flung, or flanged as my old dad might say, the bottle in question. The Berriman nose, however, does seem to have been flattened in fair and square combat by our old friend, Mr. Barty Ryan."

"Boy, some to-do," whistled Bugden. "Any body else we know mixed up in it?"

"I'm so glad you asked, Constable. You'll be delighted to hear, especially you, Cyril, I'm sure, that we are hosting this morning, not only our dear friend Barty, but also our most dedicated and frequent customer, the infamous Mr. Mutt Benoit, along with, as no doubt you've already guessed, his faithful sidekick, the esteemed Fob Stuckless. All three a bit frayed around the edges, to say the least."

Burns hunched massive shoulders in sympathy, but they both knew that with the Yanks involved they would have to go strictly by the book.

"And now for a real surprise, gents. You're going to find this hard to believe, but take a guess. How much cash do you suppose we found between the four of them? Go ahead, take a guess, keeping in mind now that we are talking about Gerry and Bart and Mutt and Fob."

Short shrugged. Busfare to Curling? "Two bucks," hazarded Bugden?

Burns paused for dramatic effect, running blunt fingertips over his stubbled jaw. "Over SIX HUN-DRED dollars, gentlemen. I repeat — over SIX HUNDRED dollars! Yes, you may well whistle in surprise, boys, I did myself when Organ showed me. Six hundred and seventeen dollars and thirty-nine cents to be exact about it. I expect Charlie will take some notice of that figure, don't you, Cyril?"

Short, much the junior sergeant, was seeing in his mind's eye the wives and offspring of their overnight detainees. Barty's wife Marilyn, eyes looking as if they'd been burnt into her face with live coals, three of four youngsters in God-alone-knew what shape, half-fed and half-clothed at best. The wives of Mutt Benoit and Fob Stuckless footing along the Curling Road early of a Sunday morning, on the way to Mass, a brood of ragamuffins herded before them. Saddest of all, Annie Tucker. Beauty and the Beast. "Too bad we can't just hand it over to the kids," he mused idly, a sentiment to which the others nodded stoic agreement. Burns snapped the occurrence book shut, capped his Parker pen and stood up, stretching mightily. "All yours then, Cyril. I'm off for a nap and then and hour or two at Steady Brook with Tommy Coombs. I suppose you heard about your pal's big catch yesterday?"

"Who? Pottle, you mean?" He and Burns were both fervent salmon men.

"Thirty-one pounds is what I heard. Biggest one of the year if it was. Over an hour-and-a-half it took before Max Rabbitts gaffed it for him. And you know what? I hear it was one of those Lee Wulff white ones did it again. White Wolf with a touch of green in it, Max told me."

"Spot of green, eh? I'll keep that in mind, Harry. Good luck to you." Short took Burn's still-warm seat behind the worn oak desk, reopened the occurrence book and entered the time of day and date in his small neat hand. The time to six o'clock stretched before him like a deserted plain, empty, parched and unwelcoming. Something green, indeed. The wooded hills along the Lower Humber were green, dark cool green where the salmon pools ran deep and clear and amber.

"I don't suppose they'd be any good for mackerel, would they?" Bugden wondered slyly. "I mean your wolf things, Sergeant?" The constable, as Short well knew, generally limited his fishing to the salt waters of the Humber Arm, with it's greater certainty of a catch of some sort. He ignored the question, recalling with distaste that Bugden was one of those new breed of 'sportsmen' who used fiberglass rods and weird-looking reels, metal lures and plastic things with a dozen hooks and spinners and God-knew-what-else on them, even worms if all else failed. He took some comfort from knowing the constable's likes wouldn't be found flailing about on a scheduled river. At least, not legally.

"Following up on that break-in at Sela's, Constable?"

Bugden nodded, and fished a notepad out of his tunic pocket. "Report on the way, Sarge. Let's see. Three dozen or so watches, rings and other stuff taken. Old Sid is making up a list, four to five thousand in all he figures. Of course, from what happened last night I expect we got a pretty good idea of who's behind that caper, right?"

"Perhaps. I see it was Gerry Tucker had the six hundred on him. Imagine. Thirty brand new twenty-dollar bills. The question, though, is where the hell would he lay his hands on such a sum?"

"Well, I think you should have a chat with Sid Sela, Sarge. You or Sergeant Burns. All that stuff just left out in the front window like that, and not a bar to it or anything."

"Trusting soul, Old Sid," Short agreed sarcastically. "See if you can find out about the insurance, too, will you? Reg Fradsham would probably know who's covering it. Probably himself." He looked up as Harry Burns reappeared unexpectedly in the squad room doorway. "Okay, Constable, you might as well get on with it then. Just make sure you're back by ten, right? Forget something, Harry?"

Burns put a finger to the side of his crooked nose and waited until Bugden had cleared the room. "I forgot to tell you, Cyril. Your friend Clive Lilly called last night. Did he manage to get hold of you at all?"

Short shook his head, wondering why Burns had bothered to come back to tell him something so inconsequential. Clive Lilly was the Assistant Post Master and worked in the building next door, the same building that housed the magistrate's court. But Burns had come across the office and was leaning in a conspiratorial manner over the desk.

"Back on it, is he, Cyril? Clive?"

"Don't think so, Harry. Been on the wagon for quite a spell now. Why do you ask?"

Burns shrugged, shaking his untidy head skeptically. "Well, just the way he sounded, that's all. He was talking sort of wild, you know, and I think he was in tears, to be truthful. But he insisted on talking to you so I figured it wasn't any emergency or anything. What with all the stuff going on here last night …"

Short regarded his fellow sergeant's broad rough face with its twice-broken, ill-mended nose, the wiry black scrub of overnight stubble on the flushed jowls. Curiosity was writ large thereon. "I'm sure it's nothing serious, Harry. They've been through a lot lately, Clive and Sybil, with that baby thing and all."

Still, it had not been a bad thing, as far as Short was concerned, that creature dying. A blessing in disguise, truth to tell. Horrible little creature, mongoloid or whatever it was, swollen head, purple-veined. It could have gone on living for years, and to what end? Lives blighted to no purpose.

"Yes, yes. I suppose so," said Burns, with a sniff of disappointment. "Anyway, just thought you ought to know, that's all. I mean, if there was anything I could do …"

"Thanks, Harry. And good luck again with the fish. Leave one or two to me now, won't you?"

He might drop in to see Clive later on, if Clive didn't come over to see him first. Meanwhile, there were charge sheets to be finished off for the crowd downstairs, and by ten sharp if the Old Sculpin was to be kept reasonably satisfied. Delays of only minutes, procedures overrunning allotted time-spans by mere moments, were complained of endlessly and querulously by The Honourable Charles Laing. A bit too old for it now, everybody said, poor old Charlie, a sentiment Short reluctantly had to agree with. Ought to be replaced, Charlie ought, but there it was, and you had to work with what you had.

Charge sheets first then, and then, time permitting, one or two other reports to be moved along. And, of course, the letter from St. John's on the Constable Organ affair, early reply expected on that one. Messy business. Bloody fool the young officer had been. He should ring up Bill French out in Lark Harbour, too. While he may have been trained by the Mounties, French was not, in Short's opinion, up to anything out-of-the-ordinary, like dealing with the Canadian Navy on an attempted murder charge. Paperwork, paperwork, he sighed. It seemed the more he did, the more he had to do. Now where in hell had Burns put the copy paper?

At ten sharp, the Old Sculpin was scowling down on the trio lined up before the bench. And a sorry looking lot they were, too, Short was thinking. Mutt Benoit and Fob Stuckless looked especially shopworn, almost fragile in a strange sort of way. Getting too old, Short realized suddenly, that's what it was, they were just like the magistrate, getting too old for it. What did the charge sheets show? Richard Benoit: age 48. And Francis Stuckless, by God, the poor fellow was all of 55. Even Barty Ryan, the youngster of the bunch, was still ripe enough at 42.

"Who's first then, Sergeant Short? Ah, Mr. Ryan. Up to our old ways again I see, Mr. Ryan."

"Yer Honner," protested Barty, with well-honed earnestness, "we didn't start nothing, now that's the honest truth of it, Yer Honner."

"Of course not, Mr. Ryan, of course not." The Magistrate's sarcasm was not the least bit pleasant, nor was it meant to be. "But the trouble is, Mr. Ryan, that we have this complaint against you made by Mr. Doucette, owner of The Caribou Inn, you see. And statements by Constables Organ and Murphy and so on. And several eyewitnesses, I understand, who can be called on to testify if you insist …"

Etcetera. The Old Sculpin was in fine fettle, and the same thing, more or less, followed with Mutt and Fob. *It was them Yanks, Yer Honner, we was only having a quiet ale when this redheaded feller ups and calls Gerry Tucker a, well, a bad name he give him Yer Honner, and that's what started it all off and what else could Gerry do when he was called a so-and-so like that?* Etcetera, etcetera. Innocent as newborn lambs, the lot of them. And the funny thing was, it seemed to Short, listening with resigned skepticism, was that there really was a sort of innocence to it all. Predictable they were, and even comic, Barty and Mutt and Fob, no threat to the established order of things. How did the old song go? Birds in cages, more to be pitied than censured? Trapped in cages they had built for themselves. Not gilded though. And if only there weren't the children and wives. That's where innocence ended.

"I'll let you make your way home now, gentlemen, because the police have more enquiries to make and some loose ends to tidy up. But I want you back here, sober mind you and straightened up — make sure you are now — on Friday next, ten in the morning, ten o'clock sharp. Is that clear to you all now? Very well. Now then, and what's the story on all this money, Sergeant Short?"

Short read from Harry Burns' manifest list,

squinting at the rough script. "Held as follows, Your Honour:

    Mr. Stuckless — $ 0.10,

    Mr. Benoit — $ 0.76,

    Mr. Ryan — $ 6.75,

    Mr. Tucker — $ 609.78

For a grand total of $617.39 in all. As you know, sir, Mr. Tucker had to be taken to the hospital for some medical attention. I understand a broken jaw is suspected as result of his having been struck with a bottle."

"I see. Bottle of ale, was it?"

"Well no, Your Honour. Actually, it was a half-full bottle of hard stuff, according to witnesses. There's no mention of what sort."

"I see. Hard stuff, you say. In the Caribou. Now what will Mr. Doucette have to say about that, I wonder?"

What could the poor fellow say, Short wondered to himself. Was he expected to carry out body searches on the boozers? Not a tavern from Humbermouth to Petries where hard stuff wasn't as common as India Pale Ale. Rum, whiskey, gin, bottles in brown paper bags, pocket flasks in jackets and overcoats, thermos-fulls in lunch pails and backpacks. Bourbon, too, with so many Yanks around.

"Well, give them their bit of change then, Sergeant. And be sure to keep me posted on Mr. Tucker's situation, won't you. And where all that cash came from. Now don't you three be forgetting about next Friday, and be sure to behave yourselves in the mean time."

Short led his sorry trio back to the station, signed them off, gave Fob a quarter for bus fare out of his own pocket and watched them shuffle out the door. No one had a clue, of course, about where or how Gerry Tucker had come into such wealth. Having a fortune like that was hard for them to even imagine. A hundred bottles of screech? More than a hundred? Case piled upon case of ale, higher than the pulpwood stacks at the papermill?

Bugden, shaking his head after the 'three musketeers', poked his head around the doorway. "Oh, Sergeant, there's someone waiting to see you in the Small Room. Clive Lilly's wife"

"Clive?"

"No, not him, it's the missus. It's Mrs. Lilly."

"Sybil? Here? " "Yes", Bugden confirmed with a vigorous nod, "it's the missus. Wants to see you, Sergeant. Alone, she says."

Sybil. Here of all places. Not just an unusual thing for her to do but for some reason it seemed to him an ominous thing. "Keep your eye on things for a bit, Constable. Did she say anything else at all?"

She wouldn't have, of course, especially not to Bugden. Short went into the washroom first, inspecting himself in the speckled mirror hung over the worn wash basin. Forty-two in three months, tired-looking eyes, copper's eyes, overused. Not a bad face, all in all, as faces go, one praised by women now and then, although not lately, square and still fit looking. A serviceable sort of face, undistinguished, and not much enhanced by the neat military mustache on the upper lip. Sighing, he rinsed his hands and ran the damp palms along the greying temples. Oh well, it would have to do, that was for sure.

It was called the Small Room, although nobody seemed to know why. As large as the outer office, it looked cramped because it was used for storage, old case-files and correspondence in heavy wooden cabinets, contraband seizures, bits-and-pieces of things, official and otherwise. It was used for interrogations and the like too, conducted at an ancient writing table under a green-shaded overhead lamp. Sybil Lilly sat at the table, smoking a cigarette, legs crossed, right foot swinging nervously, or impatiently perhaps. A rain coat lay across the table, a leather handbag by her elbow. Her skirt and blouse were rose coloured, strikingly out of place in the dusty jumble around her.

"You didn't have to come here, Sybil. I mean, why didn't you just give me a call? I could have come over. What's the problem?"

Sybil shook her head, shoulder length auburn hair shining under the overhead bulb. "Clive is home today and I wanted to see you alone, if I could."

Short sat down across from her. Her voice had trembled when she spoke but there was the familiar edge of huskiness that had always entranced him. "Of course, if there's anything I can do. Is it Clive? Is he sick or something?"

She put her head back and blew smoke into the yellow glow above them. "You could say he was, I suppose, in a way. It's about her, Cyril. About Barbara."

"Barbara? You mean …the baby? The thing?"

She nodded, closed her eyes, sighing as if to ease a deep pain. "That was my mother's name, you know, Barbara. She wasn't too thrilled to have that grandchild named after her though."

"A sad thing, Sybil, and you know how sorry I am, how sorry we all are. But at least she's at rest now, isn't she? Not much comfort to you, I know, or to Clive, but it takes time to get over these things, doesn't it?"

She ground out her cigarette, angrily it seemed to Short, then fished a pack of Camels from her handbag and shook two more out onto the table top. With a shaking hand she put one in her mouth and held the other out to him. He lit them both, conscious of her dark appraising eyes over the match flame. His yearning for her, as keen and undeniable as ever, was no doubt obvious.

"Clive says …" She hesitated, drew on her cigarette and exhaled raggedly. "Clive thinks he killed her, Cyril. He keeps saying it over and over, that he killed her."

Short shook his head, his uneasiness over her showing up here at the station confirmed. "What do you mean, Sybil? Why would he say that?"

Sybil stood up, turned abruptly and went to the narrow window at the back of the room, trailing smoke in her wake. For a few seconds she stood silently, looking out on the unkempt courtyard at the rear of the station. "It was him, you know, wanted her put away. Wanted her sent into St. John's he did. Couldn't stand having her in the house, Cyril, to tell the truth."

God forgive him, but he couldn't help sympathizing with Clive. Bulging red-veined eyes, drooling purple maw, hairless. That had been Barbara, Sybil's baby. It seemed to him especially wrong and hideous, totally inexplicable that such a creature could be brought in to world by her, by his Sybil.

Sybil shuddered and gasped, as if struck by a stab of pain and Short got up and went to the window, putting a comforting hand on her shoulder. "But mightn't it have been a blessing, Sybil, that she didn't live that long? God's will perhaps, as they say?" He shook his head, listening to his own words. Nonsense he was talking, platitudes that would shame a seminarian, while the nearness, the sweet smell of her perfumed hair, made him feel slightly dizzy.

She leaned back against his chest. "I loved her,

Cyril. I really loved her. Clive couldn't understand that, he just couldn't. Oh, and I saw your face, Cyril, when you looked at her, so I know you might find that hard to understand too. But she was mine, I had her, and I loved her. And now she's dead …".

A painful tightness in his throat, Short held her shoulder, bones like the bones of a small bird trembling under his touch. His question was one he did not want to ask. "Is there something you want to tell me, Sybil? About her death?"

She drew away, turning to face him, suddenly composed and under control again. For a dreaded second it seemed to him she might say something he did not want to hear. She hesitated, but then shook her head. "No. No, I just wanted to ask you to have a talk with him, Cyril. You're his best friend, you know, his only real one come to that. But I just have to get out of the house, just have to get away for a bit. I'm going down to stay with the family for a while."

Harry Burn's comment occurred to him. "Is Clive? You know, is he hitting the bottle again?"

She sighed and nodded. "Afraid so. Out of guilt, probably, or else that's a handy enough excuse. You know how it is. All I know is I can't help him any longer and he can't help me, and I simply can't stand being in the house with him right now. Will you try, Cyril? For me, as well as for him?"

Of course he would try, he told her. He would walk on live coals, probably, if she wanted him to. "Nothing else then, Sybil? That you wanted to tell me?"

"No, I guess not, Cyril, and I can't thank you enough for doing this for me. I'd better go now if I'm going to catch the *Express*. Gene Whelan's got the taxi outside." She reached into the handbag again and took out a sheet of paper for him, her family's address in the Codroy Valley and the nearest telephone number. It was the priest's house, she said, but they would get a message to her if need be.

She might have been his but for the damn war. Her watched her take her leave, returning her over-the-shoulder smile and wave of goodbye, sitting down wearily when the door closed and letting out a long ragged sigh. If only she was his to hold and comfort. And she had not told him everything she had come to tell either, of that he felt uncomfortably sure.

Bugden was on the phone when he reentered the office. "Just hang on, Doctor." He put his hand over the mouthpiece. "The hospital, Sergeant. Bad news, I think."

Gerry Tucker was dead, Fred Pottle told him. "Seems he had an odd sort of skull fracture, Cyril, worse than we thought. I expect you'll be along, will you?"

"Christ! When did this happen, Fred?"

"About an hour ago. Somewhere between nine and ten it seems. The nurse … let's see, Nurse Rowe it was … thought he was still sleeping it off, you see, and it was only when she was making the rounds about ten-fifteen or so that she realized what was up. He'd been checked at nine-fifteen and seem'd to be okay, breathing a little roughly, but nothing out of the ordinary. Too bad, Cyril."

"Does his missus know yet?"

"As a matter of fact, Reverend Loder was in here about a half-hour ago and said he'd go down Curling way to see her. Didn't know they were Church of England, did you? Anyway, I expect she knows by now. Sad business. Tell me, Cyril, he was hit with something, wasn't he? A bottle or something?"

Gerry Tucker had been hit by Life, Short thought to himself, as blunt an instrument as could be found. Thank God for the clergy, though, for taking one bit of unpleasant business off their hands. Of course, he would still have to talk to Annie Tucker, especially about all that cash. "Yes, it was a bottle, Fred. Thrown. Look, I'll be along in a half-hour or so, okay?"

He hung up, leaned back in the swivel chair and rubbed his chin, slowly absorbing the day's events. The scent of Sybil Lilly's hair lingered, as well as the growing certainty she had not told him everything about the Thing's dying. But perhaps she had, and perhaps his doubt was only the policeman's in-grown expectation of the worse. Time would tell perhaps, or perhaps wouldn't, leaving another of the many loose ends floating around in his head.

"A real shock, eh?" he said to Bugden. "Look, I'd better go along and see what's happened up there. Would you please call Captain Geller out at Harmon and tell him about Gerry's death. Have to be a damn inquest now."

"Anything else I can do, Sergeant? About the Lillys or anything?

He gave Bugden as disapproving a look as he could muster. "That's strictly private, Constable. And keep it under your hat, please, about Sybil Lilly being here."

Little chance of that, Short told himself, walking up West Street to the hospital. A born gossip, Bugden, if there ever was one. But then most policemen were nosy and curious by nature, exchangers of idle rumour and speculation. He was as guilty himself as the next one, come to that. After all, you could never know when some snippet would come in handy. Still, it had been unwise of her to come to the station like that. Desperate move, perhaps. And she might never come back either, come to that. No chance for him now. He sighed … and ached.

Disinfectant, mildly acrid, assaulted his nose when he entered the hospital. He found Fred Pottle in a consulting room off the main corridor. The dapper little Englishman sat staring idly into space, sipping tea and nibbling on a plate of cucumber sandwiches. Gladly, Short accepted a proffered cup.

"Seems straightforward, Cyril. Here, have a look at this." The X-ray showed a fine fracture line just above the left ear, clear as a pen stroke, like a hair fallen out of place. They were pretty certain, too — another doctor had a look at it — that under that fault line there was bound to be something else. "The autopsy will find it, I'm sure of that. There'll have to be one, of course."

"Yes," Short agreed, and wondered how many bottles and other blunt objects had been cracked over that thick skull during Gerry Tucker's wild career. "Damn that the Yanks are involved, too. Body will have to go into St. John's, I suppose. No doubt they'll want to have their own man on hand."

"An old trauma revisited," Pottle was saying. "I doubt if anything could have been done to save him, Cyril, even if we had known about it. And by the way, the wife is just down the hall if you want to see her. She came back with the Reverend."

The best of times to ask questions, Short knew, with defenses usually let down in times of stress — births, accidents, unexpected death. The worst of times too, of course, taking advantage of someone's bad luck. But duty was duty, and that was the policeman's lot, tidying up the loose ends of misspent lives. He drained the last of his tea and stood. "Better go have a word with Annie Tucker. I'll keep you informed about the inquest, Fred."

"Of course. Oh, and say, Cyril, do you have time for an hour or two on the river tonight? I expect you heard about my luck on Sunday?"

He'd bloody well make the time, Short said, and thought, the devil take Clive and his guilty boozing. They agreed to meet at Tommy Dunphy's cabin at Steady Brook where the doctor kept a cedarstrip fishing boat. "See you there about six-thirty. White Wolf, was it? On Sunday?"

Pottle shook his head. "An everyday Thunder and Lightning, Cyril. But Max raised two on drys. If they're taking, they're taking."

Short smiled and nodded agreement and went down the hallway to find Annie Tucker. It was still hard to believe, poor old Gerry Tucker dead from a squalid tavern brawl, sunk like a derelict ship, a wife and three kids floundering in the wake of misery left behind. Ah, well, perhaps it would turn out to be a good evening for the salmon, even for the hooking of one if he was lucky.

"Sorry about your loss, Mrs. Tucker. Would you like a cup of tea? Coffee?"

He sat down across from Gerry's widow, sizing her up as a real person for a change, not just as a shadow hovering in a shabby background. A good looking woman, he thought, worn down now, of course, but she must have been a real beauty in her day. Who had she been, he wondered, searching his memory? Who had Gerry married? West Side girl, for sure. Yes, one of the Delaney girls it had been, Annie Delaney.

"Tell the truth, Sergeant Short, I wouldn't say no

to a stiff drink right now if we had one. I just can't believe he's gone."

"Do you have any family close by?"

"I called Moira up in Deer Lake, she's coming down to help out. That's my sister, Moira Cunningham. The Reverend says he'll look after the funeral and all that. I don't have any money even to bury him, not a penny."

He explained to her about the autopsy requirements, all the while aware of how she was sizing him up, calm and calculating. Under control she was, a touch of steel under the fluttering surface. Like Sybil Lilly.

He hesitated. "Look. Annie … may I call you Annie? Look, I don't want to raise this right now but I'm afraid I have to. You see, Gerry had some cash on him when he was taken in last night. Quite a bit of cash, actually."

She did not look surprised, he thought, not at all surprised. "Cash? How much cash, Sergeant?"

"He had six-hundred dollars on him, Annie. All in brand new twenties."

She caught a stray straw coloured lock between two fingers and patted it back over her left temple. It took her a few seconds to respond, to absorb, perhaps, what she had been told. "Six-hundred dollars? Gerry?"

"Do you have any idea how he could have come into that sort of money? A bundle like that, all new bills?"

He watched carefully and decided she knew something about it all right. He could sense that in the way she slid her eyes away, the clasp of her long thin hands in her lap. He would bet a month's wages on it, that she knew where and from whom Gerry Tucker had got his hands on such a small fortune. But at the same time it seemed to him that she was also taken aback by the amount involved. "Six hundred," she said, as if talking to herself. "Do I get that then, Sergeant? Now that he's dead?" A note of alarm crept into her voice. "They won't take it for the funeral, will they?"

"Did Gerry say anything about some jewelry, Annie, do you recall? Was he in possession of anything like that? Stuff he was trying to sell, maybe?"

She regarded him calmly with grey-blue eyes, shaking her head with a small smile. He couldn't help smiling back. Stress would be no help in tackling Annie Tucker, that was plain to see. He prodded with a few more questions but she was totally in control. Steel.

"I expect your sister will be along in a minute or so. Again, I'm really sorry about Gerry."

She nodded and thanked him. "You used to play baseball, right Sergeant? I remember you, Cyril Short. For the West Side? They used to call you Shortstop Short. Right? You must remember how good Gerry was at it. There wasn't anybody could hit as good as him, or chase the fly balls. And we always had a chance against the Americans if he was on the team."

Of course he remembered. They'd been on the same team for two or three years and Gerry Tucker had been as close to being a real pro as a local player could expect to be. The Yanks from Stephenville were always telling him he should try out down in Florida and were more than half-serious about it too. But they might as well have talked to Gerry about taking up residence on the Riviera.

"Couldn't stay off the booze," sighed Annie Tucker. "That was his downfall." She shook her head in regret, then reached out to touch Short's arm. "I hope I can get that money, Sergeant. Will you do what you can about that for me? For old time's sake?

For his kids?"

He smiled reassuringly and noncommittally, patted her shoulder and went through his litany of comforting aphorisms. "Well, he's at rest now I suppose," he finished lamely, frowning inwardly. It was the second time that day he had played the stereotypical clergyman and he took his leave feeling slightly inadequate, a bit sadder and certainly no wiser.

Things were calm enough back at the station. Bugden was leaning back in the old swivel chair, feet up on the desk, reading the latest *G8 and His Battle Aces,* the cover an iron-crossed biplane falling from the sky in flames while in the background a triumphant Spad went soaring into the sun.

"Any calls, Constable?"

"Dead as a doornail, Sergeant," yawned Bugden, vacating the seat of authority. Oh yes, I got hold of Captain Geller and he'll be in tomorrow morning around nine. You can let him know if that's not a good time."

Messy business for the Yanks, Gerry Tucker dying like that. They would be very unhappy in the upper ranks, their sensitivities being what they were when it came to getting along with the natives. Not a bad lot, the Yanks, not a bad lot at all. Now those damn Canucks off the corvettes, there was a mean bunch when they'd had a snort or two.

Bugden cleared his throat dryly two or three times, a sure sign he was about to raise a delicate matter. "I don't suppose anything is decided yet, is it, Sergeant? About Bob?"

The letter from St. John's lay imperiously in a locked drawer of the desk. There was no profit in putting things off, Short knew, and Harry was even worse than he was trying to fob it all off on his shoulders. "I don't know what Sergeant Burns has in mind, Constable, and we really haven't had time to deal with it yet. A damn fool thing, showing off like that. Damn foolish."

"Nobody got hurt or anything all the same," Bugden pointed out needlessly. Short was aware that Bugden and Constable Bob Organ were close personal friends as well as comrades-in-arms. "Just careless he was, Sergeant, could have happened to any one of us."

Short unlocked the desk drawer and took out the dreadful envelope. "You see this letter, Constable? Straight from the Inspector General's office, my friend, right from the top this is. They've heard right from Jack Lush himself, you see, with all the gory details. That shot ricocheted right off a pail on his back porch and it scared the living daylights out of him, especially since his nerves are pretty ragged at the best of times after the stuff he went through in the first war. And who knows, an inch or two either way and it might have hit one of those kids, and then wouldn't your friend be in trouble. Not that he's not in enough trouble as it is."

God alone knew how many souvenirs like Constable Organ's Enfield were laying around in chests and drawers all over Newfoundland. Like ticking time bombs they were, and it was only a matter of time before something like this happened again with, God forbid, even more serious consequences. That was the way of it with firearms, especially with pistols, fascinating men, young boys especially, and then going off from time to time. It had been an accident, of course, everybody knew that, the Inspector General knew that and the Head Constable knew it, Constable Organ showing off to the neighborhood kids. A very human accident, even comical in a restrained way, potentially at least, except of course to Jack Lush. But the problem in this case was that it wasn't just anybody. It was Constable Robert Organ of The Royal Newfoundland Constabulary, and he simply wasn't allowed to have accidents involving firearms.

"Only an accident," Bugden offered weakly. "He's a good man, Bob is."

That he was, Short agreed. It was Organ, with a hand from Constable Murphy, who had cleared up that mess at The Caribou last night, and had made a good job of it too. He had also had the presence of mind, in the middle of all the hullabaloo, to send Gerry Tucker to the hospital. Very messy business it would have been if he had kicked the bucket downstairs. Perhaps they could get him off with a reprimand, at worst, a suspension. "We'll do our best for him. Now then, how did you get on with Sid Sela?"

"I didn't get to see Sid," said Bugden, shaking his head. "In bed with the migraine, according to his missus. Had a chat with the son, though, with young Sid, who was home on a visit from Nova Scotia. He gave me a list of what was taken. About five thousand worth."

Young Sid? Now that Bugden had mentioned it, Short recalled reading something in the *Western Star* about the son 'opening his own shop in Dartmouth, following in the family tradition,' as the paper put it. "Interesting, Constable. What do you think?"

"First thing I thought of. Trouble is, Young Sid left on the *Express* this morning and, well, I didn't think there was anything we could do. I haven't got anything on the insurance angle yet."

Short shook his head. Bugden was probably right and there just wasn't enough to go on to justify holding Young Sid, or even to make a search. All they needed now was another complaint from the Selas, on top of the Organ affair. So there it was, the train rattling away to Port-Aux-Basques, bearing Young Sid Sela and perhaps — but only perhaps — a bagful of goodies. Bearing her away, too, Sybil, with her own bagful of guilt and sorrow.

The constable left to do his afternoon walk along Main Street and Short started on the burden of paperwork, grateful for once that there was a legitimate excuse to put off answering the letter from the IG. With any luck it would be a quiet night and the senior sergeant would have no choice but to make a start on that mess. He was in the middle of writing up the Tucker affair when Harry Burns himself, freshly uniformed but nonetheless looking a bit weary, made his appearance. Almost five already, Short realized, and he had not even managed a bite of lunch for himself. "Well, any luck, Harry?"

Burns shook his head. "A few raises. They're there right enough, hundreds of them, just not taking worth a damn. And Lord, Cyril, I just heard about Gerry Tucker. By Jesus, I'll tell you I'm glad we didn't shove him in the cell last night with the rest of them. Poor old Gerry, eh? He didn't deserve to end up like that though, you know."

Shakespeare, Short couldn't help thinking, would have it all wrong when it came to Gerry Tucker. Only the good would survive this burial, the way everybody was going on. Still, not a mean sort, Gerry, whatever Bugden might think of him, just befuddled most of the time, pursued by the bottled demons. Certainly not the sort to go about smashing in store windows. Out of character that would be, unless, of course, somebody put him up to it. Well, they could only speculate. The *Express* would have pulled into Port-Aux-Basque by now, Young Sid Sela safe-and-sound on the ferry. And Sybil would be back in the bosom of her family in Codroy, and back too, probably, in the bosom of her old church.

They discussed the day's events briefly, Burns agreeing there was nothing to be done about the Sela break-in as far as Young Sid was concerned. No doubt the insurance people would have something to say on the business and that might lead to something. There would have to be a follow-up on the Lark Harbour shooting and a start on the Constable Organ file too, Short reminded him.

"So your green bit didn't do much good after all, Harry? Well, Fred and I will be giving it a try in an hour or so. Glad you left one or two fish for us."

Burns made a sour face and waved his junior on his way, contemplating the wasted hours on the river and the long pitiless night stretching ahead of him. With Sergeant Hogan on leave he had, in a fit of greed and need, volunteered for double shifts, an impulse he was beginning to regret. Still, with a quiet time of it he might be able to grab a catnap come midnight. "It's all luck, my son, it's all luck," he said to Short's back.

At six o'clock, fishing gear on, tea and ham sandwiches digesting peacefully, Short was on the road, enjoying the showroom smell of his new Pontiac, relishing a sensation of freedom. An illusion, to be sure, but one worth indulging in, even for a few fleeting hours. Once past the gravel pits in Humbermouth he could really relax, taking in the green of the river valley, the sheer purple cliffs. Within the hour he was with Fred Pottle in the doctor's cedarstrip fourteen-footer, anchored at the head of the great salmon pool, formed where the sluggish waters of Steady Brook entered the swift-flowing Humber.

"Life can be good sometimes, eh, Fred?" At times like this, here on the great seaward flood, the rosy-shanked hills rising above them to the north, Short was inclined to indulge a penchant for expounding on existential matters, a habit which Pottle, who had long ago given up concerning himself with such bothersome matters, did nothing to encourage.

"Oh, He, or She, or It, is on side now and then, Cyril, I suppose. What are you using there?"

Short had opted for a long-shanked Green High-lander. He had decided to try a spot of green after all, although he had been given to understand that the fish were colorblind at best. Pottle had tied on his favourite, a Jack Scot, pale rosy neck feathers but totally greenless. They cast, pipes alight, for an hour or so with no luck, changing flies two or three times. A dozen fish jumped in that time and Short was sure he had raised a grilse right at the head of the pool. "They're getting ready to move up in the dark," said Pottle. "I'm going to switch one last time, try out that otter hair Max made up for me. One last try."

But it was not to be. Dusk fell quickly, the last sunlight brilliant on the sheer cliffs. They relaxed, puffing aromatic smoke, watching it waft away like incense over the rushing stream, throwing long futile casts with practiced ease. An angler downstream, thigh-deep off the pebbly shore, reeled in and clumped his way to dry land, defeated for the day.

"Oh yes," said Short, breaking a long contented silence. "There was something I wanted to ask you. You looked after Sybil didn't you, Fred? Sybil Lilly?"

Pottle took the briar out of his mouth, frowning slightly, and tapped the bole against the cedar stripping. "You know very well I did, and that strictly speaking I can't really talk to you about it. But what in the world brought this into your head all of a sudden?"

Short told him about the morning visitor, what Sybil had said to him about Clive blaming himself for the child's dying. "I'm just trying to figure out why he'd have such a notion at all, let alone strong enough to drive him back on the booze."

Pottle rubbed his chin, regarding Short speculatively. "First of all, is this any sort of police business, Cyril?"

Short shook his head. "I don't think so. No. She asked me to have a talk with Clive, that's all, which I plan to do later on tonight."

Pottle nodded in sympathy. "It turned them inside out, of course, the child being like that. Brain damage, spinal cord not right either, poor little creature. I always hope they'll be stillborn or survive for just an hour or so. Well, but there it is, Cyril, it just happens. Genetics perhaps. Or bad luck."

"How long would you expect something like that to live, Fred, normally?"

Pottle gave Short another long appraising look. "Should I know why you're pestering me with these questions, Cyril?"

He could understand Pottle's hesitation. There was, he had to admit, a policeman's touch to his questioning, but it was only official curiosity so-to-speak. Nothing would ever come of it, of that he was certain. "As I said, I've got to go see Clive Lilly tonight, and I need all the ammunition I can get, Fred. Sybil's left him, you see, gone back to the Codroy, and I'm puzzled why something like this would drive them apart instead of bringing them closer together. She said Clive wanted to send the baby into St. John's, wanted to get rid of it you might say. Is that what's making him feel guilty, do you think?"

Pottle switched to a cigarette, flicking a still glowing match into the stream. A fish leaped and fell back heavily into the riverflow. "And I was happy to arrange it for them too, Cyril. Except Sybil was dead against the idea, dead set against it."

Her profession of love for her lost child echoed in Short's memory. He made a half-hearted cast in the general direction of the last fish that had broken water. "You weren't surprised in any way, Fred? By the way things turned out?"

Pottle now looked clearly exasperated, and Short knew he had gone as far as he could. "I had no trouble signing the death certificate, Cyril. Look, that's my last word on this subject, okay? And as far as I'm concerned, this conversation never took place."

Short smiled reassuringly, put down his rod, and began pulling up the small anchor. "What conversation is that, Fred?" As a policeman he knew that most human screw-ups didn't have neat tidy fixes. People did the best they could, did what seemed right and then repented and tried to repair at leisure, so-to-speak. Clive had to be helped, Sybil had to be helped. It's what friends and lovers were for, after all. And at the same time a heavy certainty had settled in his heart. Her stay in the Codroy Valley would be a long one. And she was now a different Sybil, forever changed.

He set the oars and rowed them shoreward. Pottle

leaned forward and patted his knee. "We must learn to be stoics, Cyril, we doctors and policemen. Don't you agree? Else, how could we stand to be fishers of salmon, eh?"

It suddenly occurred to Short that he could, and totally above board, simply hand over that cash to Annie Tucker. Hadn't The Old Sculpin said to give them their bit of money back? *Stupid of me, Your Honour, indeed it was, but I assumed you meant all of it, you see, Gerry Tucker's included.* A few sparks might fly, a few eyebrows raised. He really is getting too old people would say, old Charlie Laing, confusing the constabulary like that. And a list of serial numbers would be just as good as evidence, if evidence was ever needed, which was at best doubtful. He thought fleetingly of Young Sid Sela, seaborne, far too far-and-away now from the not overly long reach of the Royal Newfoundland Constabulary. It would help to balance things out a bit, tip the scales against all the heavy things of the world.

Short smiled to himself. Stoic be damned.

# TRAVELLER

H er mum gives her money for the Friday-night show at the Palace, enough to pay for herself and Mary Byrnes too, but of course they walk along Broadway right past the movie house, heading for Johnson's Ice Cream Parlour where they can buy Cokes, flirt with the boys and mooch a cigarette or two if they get lucky. They are almost there when a taxi draws up across the road and beeps and Gene Whelan, Mary's first cousin, the one who had been kicked out of St. Bernard's for some reason or other, sticks his head out the driver's side and calls them over.

Did they want to go to the St. Paddy's Day dance over at the White House?, he asks them, offering them Royal Blends at the same time and going on about the great band the Yanks had flown in from the States, just for this one time and what a shame it would be to miss out on it. Her mother would kill her if she ever knew she'd gone near the USO, but she agrees because Mary wants to go and, anyway, Gene promises to have them home safe-and-sound by ten-thirty at the worst. They are dressed up a bit after all, good enough for a time at the White House anyway, but would they be let in? Weren't you supposed to be at least eighteen and the two of them barely turned sixteen, although Mary looks old enough for sure, and she wasn't that far behind herself.

They needn't have worried. Some girl, luckily not a local, just takes Gene's tickets at the door and doesn't even give them a second look. And there they are, right in the middle of it, with the famous band playing a hit parade dance number, coloured lights sweeping over the dance floor, couples swinging and gliding about, the clink of glasses and chatter and laughter all around. Gene buys them each a Coke, the real stuff too, he assures them, right in from the *US of A*, and sneaks a little something into the glasses from a flask, a bit of a lift he calls it, screech most likely, and they can't help laughing because just then the band starts playing *Drinking Rum and Coca Cola*. She has to drain her drink because this really good looking airman asks her to dance with him, and she does because she loves to dance and is naturally good at it. Then Gene gives her another Coke, with no screech please she tells him, but there is, and then this really dreamy looking Yank takes her arm and leads her out to do a Glen Miller tune. After that Gene gives her another Coke and then she's off again, this time with a really nice looking guy with blonde hair who tells her his name is Ray and he's from California and that she's the prettiest girl on the floor, for sure. To this day she can't tell how she ends up in the back seat of Gene Whelan's taxicab or if she is with Ray from California or someone else, but she lets him, whoever it is, take off her panties and then she does it, and it's not rape like her Dad says, because the truth is she wants to, and she lets him do whatever he wants to do.

Four months ago that was. Well, almost four. How the time is flying. And now she waits and watches — it seems to her a stranger waits, somebody not her, living in her body, in a house where she is now a stranger herself.

The Malhams live on Burke's Road, a graveled laneway running uphill from Broadway, the West Side's main drag. Looking northwards over the tarry roofs of their neighbours, she has a clear view of the

Humber Arm, its ruffled waters slate-blue today under a cool July sky. *The Manchester Queen* should be outward bound this morning, according to the *Western Star*, and she was hoping to catch sight of the paper-carrier as it leaves the bay, flags and bunting fluttering, the great white forecastle proud and triumphant, a great spirit freed at last from the restraint of moor line and anchor. The *Star* must have it wrong though, it's after one o'clock and she's been watching since eleven-thirty with only the odd dory to be seen putt-putting about in mundane busyness.

With a sigh she straightens the chenille curtains and turns to regard herself in the dresser mirror. Not much to see there either, not unless you took special notice and knew what a slim one she had been. Her Mum might be wrong and she wouldn't swell up like a balloon after all, like Vera Wiseman next door, although it was still early days and the big thing, of course, is that there's a husband next door too, so Vera Wiseman can get as big as a blimp if she wants to, and still go to Mass of a Sunday. She touches her left cheek, still tender from where her Dad's backhand had landed, the blow half-checked but enough to send her backwards onto the front room couch. Three or four times he'd cuffed at her, bruising her forearm when she tried to fend him off, and God knows what he'd have done if her mum hadn't managed to calm him down. To think he could get so livid with his little Jenny, his one and only precious jewel. *To My Precious Jewel Jenny Sweet Sixteen* he had written on her birthday card. The worst thing is she couldn't tell them much. She really couldn't recall too much truth to tell, except that they had gone to the dance and perhaps she might have had a drink, she wasn't sure.

Yes, Mary Brennan had been with her but it wasn't her fault or anything, and she didn't dare say a word about Gene Whelan.

The hollow distant sound of a ship's horn calls her back to the bedroom window, but there is still nothing to see. She has heard that ships will do that sometimes just to call back any of the crew that might be tardily ashore: *Where are you? Where are you? I'm ready to leave, hurry-up, hurry-up.* The sound seems to echo over and over in her head and she wishes she could be one of that tardy lot, to go sailing out to the gulf, across the broad Atlantic perhaps, or to the far Caribbean, the town behind her forever, everything left behind forever.

She sees the black sedan turn off Broadway but keeps her eyes on the distant waters of the bay. A minute passes and she turns again to the dresser to brush her hair into some semblance of order. She hears the fuss at the front door and the murmur of voices in the front room and then her mum coming up the stairs. "It's Father Callaghan," says her mother, her pale resigned countenance reflected in the mirror over her shoulder. "I suppose you better come on down, Jenny."

That was two weeks ago. Three, almost. Time is flying. You'd still never tell though, not just by looking at her casually. The best thing is there's no longer a stranger in her mirror or in her body because there is nothing now to wait for, everything is decided and settled, only time to pass by as it surely will.

The August day is overcast and cool, so she can wear a light fall coat without drawing attention to herself. Her Mum sits on a bench in front of the station, icicle stiff and brittle, while her Dad fusses inside over tickets and seats and her trunk. Jenny stands behind her Mum, looking over the railway yard at a few boxcars and pulpwood-piled flatcars, fat clouds of steam boiling out of the paper mill's stacks, a dory glimpsed at the wharf beyond. She takes in the soiled prow of one of the paper-carriers moored at the newsprint warehouse, notes the rust-streaked age-worn forecastle. The *Foreign Express* is running a bit behind someone has told them, but has gone through Deer Lake and won't be long now, lots of time to make the eight-o'clock ferry, and of course they wouldn't be sailing without the *Express* anyway.

"Well now, Genevieve Malham. And it's off to the mainland school then, are we now?" Jack Power, the Station Master, has come up behind her and the sound of his voice makes her start. Family friends the Powers are, himself and her Dad both from Bonavista Bay, with the whole family coming by for Sunday dinner now and again. She tries to read in his face if he knows the truth of it and decides, yes, something in the way of his standing there in his dusty shiny-kneed serge, something in the very stance of the man, persuades her that he knows all right, or has guessed. Thank God her Dad comes bustling up at that moment because she doesn't know what she can say, what is there in Jack Power's eyes. Pity, or something worse.

"Oh yes, she's off to give it a try, Jack. Eh, Jenny?"

Jack Power smiles and nods. Oh indeed, a grand thing to do he agrees, from what he's heard it's the very best schooling to be got at that place. Oh yes, if only he could afford it himself, and it's fear, Jenny realizes, in his eyes, that's what it is. His own precious little jewel to worry about after all, his little Irene, only thirteen yet, mind you, but all the same. "So, and is

Sheila going up too, Frank? Making a holiday of it?"

No, no, not feeling up to it at the moment, Sheila isn't, not at all herself lately. Too busy too, at the store and all. "Sure, and Jenny's a ... well, she's practically all grown up now sure." A 'big girl' now he had started to say, yes, and getting bigger by the day she is sure Jack Power is thinking to himself. Besides, her Dad rambles on, "Sister Imelda is on her way up to the very same convent school, would you believe it now, going up on the very same train that very same day, and has offered to see Jenny delivered safe and sound." "Well now, a lovely bit of luck that is," says Jack, and her Dad says, "Oh yes, it certainly is." A great relief to them as Jack could well imagine. "Want her to have a few weeks too, you know, before the school starts, getting used to the big city and all that." Jack Power nods to her Dad, nods and smiles at her.

Jenny sits down next to her Mum. A reluctant sun has broken through the overcast and the untidy scene before her seems unreal in the cool afternoon light: railway cars, roiling clouds of steam, the steely-blue glimpse of the bay waters. Her Mum's silent pain and her own simmering excitement are the only things that seem real at all, everything else as false and transitory as Jack Power's smile. Suspended the world seems to be, timeless, like when the projector breaks down in the middle of a show and the film freezes on the silver screen.

Dreamily the *Express* finally rounds Humbermouth Point and Jenny watches it chug its slow clangorous way to the station. Her Mum melts, grips Jenny's hand so hard it makes her wince. "Oh Jenny," her Mum cries, eyes awash, kisses cold and hard on Jenny's cheek, "Oh, Jenny." Then her Dad, and he doesn't know what to do either, poor man, touches her shoulders, pecks at her cheeks, drops his arms, slaps his thighs, clasps his rough hands, sighs and sighs again with great puffs of air. "Well, well now," he says, "well now." They peck at each other, squeeze arms and hands, tell each other she'll be just fine, no need to worry at all, not at all. Thank God when it's 'All Aboard!' and she can turn away and climb to refuge in the passenger car.

Her Dad had pestered the railroad office for good seats, two right up at the front he had wanted, but as it turns out the car is practically empty and they can take a seat just about anywhere they care to. Jenny thinks she wants to sit looking ahead while Sister Imelda says she doesn't care one way or the other. The nun settles down across from Jenny and right away opens up and starts reading in her breviary, laying on the seat beside her black-robed hip a copy of *The Sunday Visitor.* She pauses to regard Jenny briefly, notes the tearful eye of her ward, decides there is nothing to be concerned about and returns to her devotions. *Keep guard over those that faithfully accept God's message, and lead back to His holy fold those that have strayed from it.* "No need for tears, my dear girl, sure you'll be home again in no time at all."

Jenny dabs at her eyes, but only nods and says nothing. Leaving — she is really, really going. Away from the sulphurous town, from all the old and in-the-past, away from those two stiff figures standing bewildered on the dusty platform, all receding, diminishing to nothing. Where would he be now, she wonders, that handsome-looking Yank, Gary, or Ray, Ray from California, the one who had touched her like that? Drinking Coca-Cola at the USO maybe, or gone altogether, more likely.

The locomotive stirs from its troubled rest, hisses and shudders and lurches into the long haul down to Port-aux-Basques and the ferry to Nova Scotia. Sister Imelda snaps shut her be-ribbonned book of devotions, takes off thick blue-tinted spectacles and turns to the window to watch the town pass by. As the *Express* escapes the woodpiles west of the paper mill and trundles past the patchwork shacks of Crow Gulch, the calm blue sweep of the Bay of Islands comes into full view. "Ah, say what you will, Genevieve Malham," she sighs, "say what you will. There's no place more beautiful than our own dear Newfoundland, my dear, no place at all."

# M O U S E

*B*arely turned twenty-one, but mature as could be. Over-ripe some thought, composed in form and manner well beyond his tender years, with not a nerve in his body, no quick to him at all. That was the book on Ambrose O'Connor. "Makes me fair nervous, that one," next door neighbour Joyce Mullins often remarked to her husband Thumper.

At *Our Mother Of Perpetual Help*, over on Caribou Road, Ambrose was never picked on. Oh, he looked bookish enough and was, in fact, serious to a fault, but the school's bullies, honing in on fear like sharks on the fluttering of a wounded fish, thought it best to give this one a wide berth. Something in the still face, the opaque eye with its unflinching gaze, gave them pause. Better safe than sorry. The Sisters, too, marked the aura of cold intent that emanated from that slight frame and, all in all, found their star pupil just a bit too self-contained for comfort.

Some wondered how he came by such uncommon self-composure at such a young age. True enough that Bernard, the dad, had been a silent one, sucking away on an unlit brier and sizing up the world around him through half-lidded eyes under a thatch of thick black brows. But, as far as could be told, Bernard had been as dull and indifferent above the shoulders as a pail of ditchwater. Taciturn and friendless, twenty years the Co-op store butcher he had been, as sullen behind his gory chopping block as a tub of leftover lard.

As for the mother, Bernice O'Connor's 'nerves' had kept her under lock and key for the last decade of her life, a time during which she could hardly bring herself to quit the little house on Watson's Road at all unless there was as inescapable and pressing need to do so. She took Nujol for cranky bowels, Dr. Chase's Nerve Food for the ups and downs, all the while spurning, scorning and slandering the local medical fraternity. When Bernard died, whatever grief there was had been more than offset by her distaste in dealing with priests and morticians and all the rigmarole of death, the ordeal of church and cemetery and strange people staring at her and saying things she didn't understand or want to hear. Truth to tell, she would sooner have had poor old Bernard wrapped up in binbags and left out for pickup at the roadside. It was all foolishness in her eyes, and she was sure she should never have consented to having Ambrose brought up as an RC. Such a nuisance with all their dos and don'ts and what-nots, although they were all the same as far as she could see — the churches, all dos and don'ts.

When her own time came, in fear of both life and death, Bernice finally called on old Doc Rowsell; but by then, as the good doctor was afterwards pleased to observe, it was far too late to do anything for her. Ambrose was barely twenty at the time and had been working at the Bank of Nova Scotia on Broadway for about two years. The bank thought highly of him, but his fellow workers, as might be expected, found him to be a bit of cold fish. It wasn't that he couldn't or wouldn't be helpful and considerate in his own way, but that everything he did, good or ill, was done in the same dispassionate manner. Banter and jokes went right over his head and you couldn't do the fellow a favour if you tried. "Fair turns you off, he does," the girls decided amongst themselves.

Nevertheless, with Bernice safely underground, Joyce

and Thumper Mullins began to size up their orphaned neighbour in a new light. "Got a nice little house now," Joyce would muse, "all to his ownself." And Thumper — the soubriquet had been earned on the soccer field with the Curling Rangers, and his real name was now so seldom used most people hardly knew he had one — would nod agreement. "And a nice little job, too," she would add. "Uh huh," he would reply, thinking, the two of them, of their niece, Clair Dingwell. Ambrose and Claire. Made in Heaven that match was.

Claire had been living with Joyce and Thumper since '43, the year her dad, Joyce's brother George, had been killed overseas and his young widow, Mina, the 'Cow Head hussy' as Joyce called her, had taken off to God Knows Where. Halifax some said, somewhere upalong at any rate, leaving the poor thing to the charity of her aunt and uncle in Corner Brook. "There's none can say we didn't do right by her," they were quick to remind all and sundry, "because we knows our duty right enough, not like somebody we could mention," although they could seldom resist naming that certain somebody, especially if Claire happened to be within earshot at the time.

Ambrose and Claire. Two of a kind they were, especially her, said Joyce, and it would take a bit of pushing and shoving that was for sure; Claire needing the push and shove more than the other one. "As backward, she is, as her mother was saucy," was Joyce's opinion; and as for him, well, at least they would have neither Bernice nor Bernard to tackle, God be thanked!

And so the targeted one, caught one evening after work in his nice little house next door, was asked around for Sunday dinner a week hence. "Now you'll just have to come, for sure," Joyce insisted " 'cause I expects you're not eating too good now, are you, not all the time, with your poor mother gone and all."

The prospect of supping with the Mullins made Ambrose squirm and he fished around desperately for an excuse that wouldn't give too much offence. He had wholeheartedly concurred with his folks opinion of the couple next door; she was common and pushy, while Thumper, perhaps not a bad fellow all-in-all, nevertheless seemed to have taken a few headers too many in his soccer career. Still, he couldn't bring himself to simply shake his head and close the door in her face, which is what Bernard would likely have done. Instead he found himself muttering something about work, a silly excuse for a Sunday night, and a poor effort Joyce easily brushed aside with a wave of her hand, going on about how it was, well, a sort of promise she'd made to her dear departed friend Bernice: keeping an eye on her poor lad and making sure he had a good four-square meal in him now and then. The audacity of the woman made him wince, but it was a better lie than he could come up with himself, on such short notice at least, so there it was — Sunday supper with the Mullins, like it or not.

"You can sit there across from Claire now, Ambrose," directed Joyce, settling them down about the kitchen table on the appointed Sabbath. Dinner was to be a fatty old hen from the Company store, stuffed with Thumper's favourite dressing of doughy white bread, raisins and sage, and served up with mashed potatoes, carrots, onions, and boiled cabbage, a jar of Joyce's sweet mustard preserve on the side. Apple pie was scheduled for dessert, hot from the oven, sprinkled with table sugar and smothered in gobs of thick tinned cream.

"How's things at the bank then?" asked Thumper, not expecting a reply apparently, because before Ambrose could even clear his throat the man was off on a diatribe against the paper mill, where he worked on the Number 4 machine and took a keen interest in union matters, especially if there was a grievance of any sort on the go. "All we wants is a decent place for a cup of tea, you should see where they makes us eat, you wouldn't put a cockroach in there. Not that there ain't enough of them ..." And so on. Thumper's World. Soon he was going on about the soccer scene, would Curling beat out the West Side, what did Ambrose think, and Lord save them, but wasn't the Hawks a sorry sight this year?

The kitchen was close, sour with the smells of onion and cabbage. Everything on his plate seemed to Ambrose to have been boiled and baked and pulverized to the point where he might just as well have been chewing on lumps of Thumper's wood pulp. Ambrose knew a thing or two about decent cooking, and this stuff wasn't even close. For starters, Bernard would never have allowed such a miserable fowl into the house; and for all her faults, Bernice had always kept a good table. Still, to his surprise, and a pleasant one it was too, he found that sitting across from Claire Dingwell was almost enough to make up for Joyce's tasteless dishes and Thumper's querulous monologue.

She sat quietly, a shy, almost secretive little smile on her lips. Not a word did she say the whole while, and he fancied she was avoiding his eye, her gaze fixed on Thumper or Joyce when they spoke but otherwise demurely lowered to her plate. It was astonishing to see how the plain little thing he had barely been aware of when she was in pigtails, and had completely lost sight of in the upper grades, had turned out to be such a pretty young woman. Had she always had those lovely grey-blue eyes and finely-wrought cheekbones, that charming sprinkle of faint freckles over the delicate bridge of the nose? Remarkable altogether, not flashy at all, not overdone with the makeup like most of them were nowadays, more sort of an old-fashioned simplicity about her, a fresh young face, framed so strikingly, too, in shiny ash-blonde locks. What would she be now? Eighteen?

"I understand you're working down at Singer's, Claire. How do you like it then?" This he managed to get in during a rare lull in Thumper's outpourings. What was the idiot on about now? Turnips?

Roses bloomed in Claire's cheeks and Ambrose felt flattered. Such a blush was surely a show of deference. "It's not too bad, Mr. O' Connor," she replied in a near whisper. "I like it well enough, actually."

*Mister* O'Connor. Imagine that, and the two of them practically the same age. What a gem was here, what a rare gem, so shy, so well mannered. "Come now, Claire, you must call me Ambrose," he insisted, smiling magnanimously.

"She gets her things half-off, too," Joyce was saying. "That blouse is pure silk, Ambrose, pure 100% silk. Go ahead, just feel it there. Hold out your arm there, Claire."

It was certainly a handsome blouse, Ambrose agreed, now that he took a good look at it — sky blue taffeta sort of thing, elbow-length sleeves with frilly fringes trimmed with small pearly-white buttons. Expensive-looking, although of course he didn't know much about that sort of thing. A fine sweep of pale blonde hairs showed on the slim outstretched forearm.

"And nice shoes, too," Joyce went on, "He don't

pay them much, Lord knows, but you can't say he don't keep his girls looking up to scratch, old Singer. They say he might be selling up soon though, now that the missus is dead."

"Goof fer buffness, m'dears, goof fer buffness," Thumper opined through a mouthful of gravy-soused potato. He rinsed everything down with a long gulp of tea to clear the windpipe. "Not out of the goodness of his heart, let me tell you."

Claire was blushing again, eyes on her plate, which she had barely touched. What a pitiful situation she must feel herself in, Ambrose was thinking, to be caught up between the likes of these two. Pitiful.

They played cards in the front room after the awful meal, but Ambrose couldn't keep his mind on the game and Thumper was soon thoroughly disgusted with his partner. "The girls is going to beat us for sure, Ambrose boy. You just trumped my queen with your jack …" But the card table was small and Ambrose couldn't help being aware of that silken shoulder, the warmth of that slim girlish body, so close to him. Her profile was perfect too; and the quiet gentle way she had about her pleased and fascinated him to distraction. He was more and more certain that the wavering smile, the quick way she dropped her eyes if he caught her looking him over, were signs of deference. She was only a shop clerk, after all, and a newish one at that, while he, on the other hand, was a full-fledged experienced Banker, a position in life which always carried a capital B in his mind's eye. Not that she was awkward or unreasonably bashful, not at all, but just naturally refined and retiring. And that blue-grey translucent look, whenever he managed to catch it, seemed to go straight to his heart.

A rare sleepless night followed. He lay staring up at the patchy ceiling of his bedroom, adding up the facts and figures of his life. The future was secure, that he was sure of. He was a born Banker if ever there was one. Looked like one, felt like one; loved the work, loved handling the bundles of banknotes and rolls of coin; proud of the way his tidy little hand could fill out the forms and ledgers so handsomely, with seldom a blot to mar them or errors to be scratched over. He was sure the bank approved of him too, that the manager thought well of him and that he was bound to be transferred up to Canada soon, to Nova Scotia most likely, but even to Toronto or Montreal perhaps. Now wouldn't a girl like Claire Dingwell, wouldn't Claire Dingwell herself for that matter, be just the perfect companion for him? Unspoiled, innocent, a flower waiting to blossom, a wife he would be proud to show off. Yes, he would rescue her. That was the very word for it too, rescue, releasing her from the prison of her unhappy circumstances, while at the same time offering her the approval and security she must surely be longing for.

A man of action when decided on a matter, the very next day he dropped into The *Empire Fashion Shoppe* where he found Claire at the back of the store hanging skirts on a rack. She was obviously more than a little startled to see him. There was this new movie on at the Majestic he rushed to tell her. *Dark Passage*, everyone was saying how good it was, and he was just wondering if she would like to see it. With him, of course.

There was that blush again, a fluttering of hands, and for a second he thought she might just shake her head 'no' out of panic. He broadened his smile as best he could. "Do you like him — Humphrey Bogart?"

he asked in a reassuring voice and was relieved when she nodded yes, and even added that Lauren Bacall was a favourite too. "That would be nice," she finally agreed, and even managed a hesitant 'Ambrose', although he fancied she had been about to address him as Mister again. He left the store in a self-satisfied state of mind.

They had a grand time at the movie. She laughed during the opening cartoon, laughter that was sheer delight to his enchanted ear. He didn't try to hold her hand, or put his arm around her, not like you'd do with an ordinary girlfriend. Too refined she was for that sort of goings on, far above it. She even put the wrapper from her *Eatmore* bar into her purse rather than throw it under the seat like everybody else. And to think he might have missed her altogether, and she living there all this time, not a stone's throw away over the picket fence.

They strolled home through a misty spring night. A full moon, wrapped in a thin gauze of cloud, hung hugely over the town. Houses, trees, hydro poles and wires, all seemed to be aglow in a hazy blue light. They chatted about the film and yes, she'd love to go to another with him, and before he knew it they were back on the West Side, strolling past the shops on Broadway.

"I hope I didn't get you into hot water at the store yesterday. You know … bothering you when you're working?"

Claire shrugged and shook her head. As it turned out, old Singer hadn't even been there at the time; anyway, he wouldn't have to do it again, would he, since she was just next door after all.

"Aunt Joyce doesn't like him at all, you know. Mr. Singer. Truth to tell, she doesn't like Jews at all the way she's always on about them. What do you think about them, Ambrose?" They were halfway up Watson's Road and she had turned her face to him in the shimmering light.

It was his turn to shrug. Well, supposed to be good with a dollar everybody said. The fact, he had to confess, was that he really didn't know any, except over-the-counter so-to-speak. Claire laughed. "She doesn't either," she said. They were at the Mullins' garden gate and she suddenly put her face close to his and kissed him lightly on the cheek. Pleasantly surprised, he watched her run into the house with a goodnight wave over her shoulder.

Another restless night followed, a whirlwind of strange emotions and uncertainties running through his suddenly feathery head. Taking his arm on the walk home, kissing him like that without even being asked, what was he to think? A strange new country seem to lay before him, risky, even dangerous most likely, but still a country, he knew in his heart, that he was bound to enter.

A dance at the Knights of Columbus followed — Thumper happened to have two extra tickets he was supposed to sell, but sure why not keep them in the family. Ambrose was finding the Mullins to be not such bad company after all, especially since he needed them to get to their darling niece. He noticed, with a nervous pride, that Claire was getting her fair share of admiring looks from the other men, young and old. And while he was normally as stiff as a salted codfish on the dance floor, he found her so light in his arms, so easily led and so footsure, he fancied he could have outdanced Fred Astaire himself that night.

Another movie, an evening of cards with Joyce and Thumper and the Howells, neighbours on the other side, and it was plain enough to Ambrose that she was his girl now, that they were a proper couple and all that sort of thing. Everybody seemed to think this was the case, and Joyce and Thumper would nod and wink at each other with open satisfaction whenever the two 'lovebirds' went out the front door. Still, Ambrose sensed in Claire a continued shyness and reserve, something he couldn't quite pin down, a something vague and uncertain that troubled his orderly mind. It kept him from even trying to kiss her, let alone entertain thoughts of a greater intimacy. It was her total innocence, of course, that kept his natural inclinations at bay, her trust that he would be the perfect gentleman in all things. Chastity, modesty — these were the great virtues he attributed to her.

After all, a real Catholic he supposed she was, not like himself, going through the old formulas and rituals out of habit. On that first date, he recalled, she had worn a little silver cross around her lovely neck, and he had observed her at Mass once or twice, bent so intensely over her missal. Besides, pleasures postponed would be all the sweeter for it, or so they said, like not opening your presents until Christmas morning.

He was soon timing his work days so he could walk her home from the store, except for those days, far too many of them in his opinion, when she would phone to let him know she would be staying late, doing inventory or fixing up a window or the like. On one early October afternoon, after receiving just such a call, he pressed her meet him, please, please, because he had such important news to tell her. She asked him to hold on a minute, returning to say old Singer had, albeit reluctantly, given her the okay to leave. When she emerged from the store he couldn't help grabbing her hand excitedly. "I've been transferred, Claire," he exclaimed. "Up to Nova Scotia, to Halifax."

She was pleased for him, she said, such a wonderful step for him, and him so young, and of course he deserved it too, had earned it she was sure. She tried a bright smile, but he could see there was something else on her mind, something bothering her. "Well, it's Mr. Singer, Ambrose. He's gone and sold the store and I suppose I'll be out of a job pretty soon."

But she smiled telling him her news, as if the prospect of losing her first ever job didn't weigh too heavily on her mind. But, it suddenly dawned on him, why should it? Wasn't she expecting to be married to him soon enough, to be going up to Canada with him, man and wife? What was her silly little job compared to that? Should he do it right now, he wondered, pop the question at that very moment? And why not? After all, wasn't that what she was expecting and waiting for, perhaps telling him about losing her job as a prompt even?

He cleared his throat, suddenly resolute, took hold of her hand again and brought them to a stop by the side of the roadway. "Claire ..." he began.

"Ambrose," she said quickly, and for a fleeting second he thought she had sensed his intent. "Ambrose, I'm taking the ten o'clock train into St. John's on Wednesday. I have to see my Aunt Bessy."

"Aunt Bessy?"

"Yes," she rushed on, "she's not well, you see, and I haven't seen her since I don't know when." She would be back the next Tuesday, even Monday if Aunt Bessy wasn't so bad. She squeezed his hand reassuringly, seeing the puzzlement on his face, and reached up to touch his lips gently with her fingertips. "It's not very long, Ambrose, four or five days. Don't look so sad, please."

They kissed and he put his arms around her, his whole being trembling. In the whole wide world, she was the only one he had wanted to tell his good news to, the one and only. *His* one and only. "And would you do me a big favour too, Ambrose, and not mention anything to Joyce or Thumper before I go. I don't know all the ins and outs of it, but Aunt Joyce and Aunt Bessy just hate each other, and I don't want to get caught up in the middle of all that."

Oh, she could trust him on that score, he assured her. It was within families that the deepest and most enduring enmities were bred and nurtured, that he knew well. Hadn't Bernard refused to go to his own brother's funeral, the two of them not exchanging as much as a Christmas card for over twenty years?

Another quick kiss, a touch on his cheek, and then she was gone. Ah well, he told himself, he could certainly wait a week or so to put the question, especially as he was confident now of the answer she would give. Her absence, too, would give him the time to buy a proper ring, one he had been eyeing in Sid Solo's window, and then to do the whole thing up properly when she got back. He touched his lips, tasting the sweetness of her mouth, the bittersweet of her lipstick. All for the best, really, all for the best.

A line of credit came through for the new owner of the Empire, who turned out to be Singer's eldest son, Ira. "He'll be chopping it back quite a bit," the manager confided. "Way overstocked, Ernie was, and way overstaffed too." So he would indeed be her hero, Ambrose concluded, plucking her from the railway track of life, from the Joyces and Thumpers of the world. How grateful she would be for that, obliged to him you could say, and that wouldn't be a bad thing at all when you added up the pluses and minuses of the thing. He bought a $200 ring from Sid Solo instead of the $100 one he'd had his eye on.

Claire did not return early. On the Monday night, Ambrose called in at the Mullins', where a grim faced Joyce led him into the front room. Thumper, she told him over her shoulder, was on the four-to-twelve shift.

"Claire's not back then? Is Aunt Bessy worse?"

Aunt Bessy, Joyce snorted. Hadn't gone near the good woman's front door, Claire hadn't. In any event, Bessy, her own dear sister, was a sound as a bell and never sick a day in her life. "That's the tale she gave you, is it?"

"I don't understand? Didn't she go into St. John's?"

"Oh, she went in all right. It's a wonder she even let us know, after letting us worry sick when she didn't come home that night." Joyce had fired up another cigarette and her words flew from her mouth in a haze of smoke and shreds of tobacco. Ambrose was certain she'd had a drop or two in the bargain. "Had to go in to get her papers, didn't she?"

"Papers?"

Joyce's angry reddened eyes looked him up and down with a mix of pity and scorn. "Oh well, I expects you got as much right to get the news as anyone else."

A wave of unease swept over him. "What news?" he asked nervously.

She laughed mirthlessly at his worried, puzzled face. "Like mother, like daughter, eh, disgracing us all like this. Here, my dear man, take a look at this." She took an envelope from a skirt pocket and handed it to him. "See that postmark there, Ambrose? Take a look at that now, will you?"

Boston? It was Boston. Boston, USA. He took

the letter gingerly from the envelope. The engagement ring — *would Sid take it back?*, he wondered fleetingly — weighed like an anvil in his jacket pocket.

*October 13, 1947*

*Dear Aunt Joyce and Uncle Thumper,*

*I am sorry to tell you like this but I am going to work for Mr. Singer in America, down in Florida. I'll let you know everything in a little while when I get settled, my new address and all. I just wanted to save trouble, because I know you don't like him and I hope I can pay you back for everything some time.*

*Love Claire*

It was, he couldn't help thinking, such a small neat little script she had, such lovely numerals and letters. Such neat columns and ledgers she would have kept. And not a mention of him, not a word, not a postscript.

"You can imagine what the job is, I'm sure," said Joyce. "Him old enough to be her grandfather. And I'm sure she's had the practice for it too, you can bet on that, my lad. Oh, you poor men. Always the quiet little ones, ain't it? Fools the lot of you, don't they?"

He handed the letter back to her and she waved him to put it on the coffee table, as if she found it unpleasant to the touch. "Takes after that one, she does, after that mother of hers. In the blood, Ambrose, in the blood. And good riddance, eh? Good riddance, don't you think?"

"I …".

He made his way back to his nice little house. Well, well now, he thought, looking at his face, white with revelation, in the dresser mirror. The ring was safely tucked away under his starched shirts in a top drawer. Might come in handy someday, yes, certainly it would. He had been sound, too, not to have rushed things with that one, to have waited for a bit. Oh, you had to be careful with them, with the girls, so careful to keep from being outfoxed or boxed into a corner.

# WHEN IN APRIL

*T*here were four staying at the Lodge that week, all white-collar specimens and, as such, quartered in the new place reserved by Mrs. Grimes for her city gentlemen types. The old bunkhouse in the back was empty: the woodmen were all in the bush and there would be nothing for the sportsmen to kill, legally at least, until mid-June.

Mr. Morry, in Room 1, travelled for B ... Bros. A peddler of hardware goods, he was on his semi-annual run around the bay and good for the whole week, even longer given a spell of rough weather on the outer shore. Adjoining him was Mr. Skimple, colporteur, (RC to the right of his suitcase, Anglican and others to the left) and settled in for an indefinite stay, trading as he did on his own time and capital. Across the hallway from his fellow travellers nestled Mr. Prior with his ancient valise and inky portmanteaus, School Inspector (Public) by trade, a twice-yearly visitor and a discomforting one for Mrs. Grimes who, no matter how hard she tried, could never succeed in making the poor fellow feel the slightest bit at home.

Lodger four, the clerk Croucher, lay on his narrow bed at two o'clock in the afternoon, a bothersome sunlight beating through the ill-curtained window on his closed eyes, his nose hanging on his puffy face like an over-ripe plum.

That organ had burst treacherously at mid-day, shooting blood over shirtfront and tie, producing a shock that had made him stagger and nearly faint. Devine, his manager, disgruntled, and by nature uncharitable towards any weaknesses in others that reminded him of his own shortcomings, had trundled him off in a taxi to the lodgings, his anger at the Main Office for supplying such low-quality relief directed openly at the pale, trembling clerk. The manager had taken an instant dislike of Croucher's pasty muffin-of-a-face from first sighting, an impression he now felt was fully justified.

At three-thirty, still feeling ill-used, Devine set the time-lock on the miniature vault and, leaving Mrs. Stirge and young Pope to finish things up, quit the bank and went to nurse his grievances nearby in the cool dark of the Bay View Inn. There he was greeted by the corpulent and deceptively drowsy- looking Oscar Rump who, while in contempt of the little red-nosed banker, still knew well enough to butter his daily bread on the upside.

"A bad day now, was it, Mr. Devine?" Rump left off inventorying his spirits and ale to settle-down the manager with whiskey and water. There was an unwashed texture to the innkeeper, a greyness of cuff and collar, and tobacco-stained teeth that could put the dapper Devine on edge. He, on the other hand, had learned to condescend at will, and a licenced vendor was not someone he cared to offend openly, whatever his appearance, especially if he happened to be the only one in town.

"There are days, Oscar, when the Good Lord himself would toss it all in."

Rump nodded. "Sure, and I feel the same way meself at times. No end to the things to be doing around here and all the goings-on. Oh, the pure misery here too betimes, Mr. Devine, pure misery."

An apt way to put it, Devine agreed silently ... pure misery, life and work and the uncaught flow of time beaching him here in this backwater, with a younger wife and only a decade to go until he was pensioned off. The thousands Rump kept fallow in the bank twisted envy in his heart, and he made a mental note to charge this visit to expenses.

"Why don't you hire on some help, Oscar? You're doing pretty well here after all."

Yes, and you're as green as a tomcod over it, thought Rump, as he topped up Devine's glass. "Ah, sure, where could I get decent help out here? Sixty miles from the city and you'd think it was the moon's backside someplace. You recall that fellow I got in here last summer?"

"Oh yes, our friend Kinslow. Whatever happened to him?"

"Last I heard he was working at the Colony up in the city." Rump chuckled in spite of himself. "Christ, but he really got around the women, eh?"

Muriel, Devine remembered, was dining at the Colony today with the city managers' wives. There was a hopeless hundred-dollar loan at the bank in Kinslow's name and he would have to remember to ask if she'd caught sight of the scoundrel. Perhaps he could get hold of the fellow's pay. "Well, it's a good thing Doc Heany didn't find him that night."

"Oh God, yes!" Rump slapped the countertop with his pudgy white hand. "He'd have killed him for sure. Coming in here with that jesus shotgun. Lord, lord!" He shook his shaggy head at the memory. "Still, she wasn't the only one who pulled them down for him, not by a long shot. Least, that's what I heard." His heavy-lidded eyes slid away from Devine's.

"Anyway, look at the trouble you get — see what I mean? And the son-of-a-bitch couldn't keep his hands off the cash either and damn near drunk more than he could put out."

"What about something local then, somebody you might know."

"Cost me a thousand, that bastard." Rump shook his head. "Naw, there's nothing good about. Get a girl and they're in trouble before they learn one drink from the other and besides, next thing you know the place gets a reputation and there goes your licence and all."

Croucher's pasty visage shot into the manager's mind. "Yes. I guess we all have our problems getting decent help, Oscar. You know that chap at the bank, Croucher, down from the city?"

"Oh sure, I know Eric Croucher. Sick again was he? Nosebleed or something?"

How much that was truly confidential, Devine wondered, did Mrs. Stirge broadcast in her daily news bulletins ? "To tell you the truth it gave me a scare, Oscar, how sick he looked. Ready for an early grave if you ask me."

Rump nodded. "Never was that healthy. His dad, you know, was the Anglican minister here around ten years back. And he was a great one too, I can tell you. Know what he did one time? Used to be an old RC church up on the hill there — where the stone one is now? Well, sir, one night she took fire, lost everything 'cept the stuff in the altar, the concentrated host as they call it, I think. Old Father Costard, he collapsed when he seen the place going up and not a soul stirring to get into her. Then the Reverend Croucher, who was only standing back in the crowd up to then, you see, jumps right into her through a side window and out he comes with the gold cup under his coat and his hair smoking and everything. I'm telling you there were those thought he was crazy, oh indeed, myself included truth-to-tell, 'cause there was no love lost in them days, eh, between the micks and the others."

"A foolish thing to do all the same," said Devine. The story had irritated him, as if young Croucher had been given unearned credentials.

"Old man's dead now," added Rump. "Young Eric come along a bit too late, I expect; near killed his mother in the bargain, as I recall. But there's lots of folk here think pretty well of him, just the same. The old reverend, I mean."

A word given to the wise, Devine thought, albeit unintentionally: the virtues of the father might well be visited on the son. "Still," he mused persistently, "I wonder at times if the new generation has what it takes, Oscar. Times are I think the whole world is going backwards on us."

"Amen to that, sir!" came a sudden voice from behind the startled Devine, "Amen to that, to my mind!" and turning he saw for the first time, seated in the sombre recesses of the dim tavern, the stiff and spartan figure of Mr. Skimple. Fresh from espousing the Church Triumphant on the Roman side of the bay, he was now into his third glass of ale, fortified, when Rump's back was facing him, with several pulls from a flask of stronger stuff concealed in his dark clerical raincoat. "Like yourself, sir, it is my long-held belief that today's young men, yes, and the young women as well, I dare say, are but shades of their fathers and mothers. Only shades, sir, pale shades."

There was a welcome elegance in Mr. Skimple's manner of speech, all the aitches in their proper places and so on, that fell pleasantly on the manager's sore ear and he felt an immediate soulship, a community of civility, with this stranger. After introductions by Rump, who was well content to be shut of them both, he joined the purveyor of religious knickknacks in a booth at the back of the room.

"To out a personal touch on the matter, my dear sir, as a personal example so-to-speak, how many people do you think would guess my own age? A double of your favourite whiskey, sir, if you can come within five years of it."

Devine felt a lift in spirits for the first time since Muriel had taken the car into the city two days ago. "Well now, Mr. Skimple, you look about fifty I'd say, or thereabouts. But on the other hand, bearing in mind that you want to wager on it, I would say, well ... oh, about sixty-five let's say."

"Oh, it's easy to see, Mr. Devine, why you have your position. Yes sir, that is calculated like a true banker, I fancy, and I do indeed. I like to think I carry my years pretty well, you'll have to agree. Sixty-five, you say? I am ... let me see now — I will be, on Friday next, eighty years old, sir, eighty ripe old years."

Devine was shaken. At fifty-five, and no way to deny it before the mirror, he had been willing to favour the rosy-cheeked Skimple with five years and a freakish constitution, but to discover him to be twenty-five years his senior? He drank quickly, fighting off a familiar flash of fear.

"A life of labour, Mr. Devine, a life of hard, hard work, from the dory to the army to school teacher, retired now, but not stopped, sir, not stopped. Never slacken, you see, that's my secret. Find a young man today, if you can, to haul the traps before sunup. A long looking you'll have I can tell you. But there's the answer, right there, right in the way we keep their noses to the grindstone. There was never a truer saying, sir, than the devil finds his own work for idle hands."

"Oh, I quite agree. Mr. Skimple, I quite agree," said Devine. "My old dad had a general store — you might recall Devine's Groceries in Brigus? And oh, I can tell you he knew how to make us sweat."

"Certainly I do recall it, yes, down by the wharf, wasn't it? And your father, too, I recall him, a fine man, a big man. Here sir, I'll make a toast for us. To our fathers, to the forefathers of Newfoundland and the hard, just rules they taught us."

Devine's glass was empty but he put it to his lips, nodding to show he shared Mr. Skimple's reverence for his shadowy progenitors. "And to you, Mr. Skimple," he added lukewarmly, "and to the next eighty, sir." Mr. Skimple's clear eye beamed at him over the rim of his glass.

The clerk, Croucher, awake by this time, had additional miseries to bear from his unruly body. The stomach was grinding out reminders that it had long since done with breakfast and had also missed its accustomed noonday scoff. The mouth, too, not used to being the sole passage to the lungs for the stuffy air in the room was coated with a bitter saltiness. The stale water in the blue pitcher next to his pillow only irritated the belly and, gingerly, he eased off the bed and went wavering in search of food.

A more handsomely gifted face, despite blood-stopped nostrils, spots, and doughy puffiness, might have drawn out a spasm of motherly concern in Mrs. Grimes. But the sight of the wrecked clerk tacking around the kitchen door like an evil spirit only rekindled the annoyance she had been nursing towards the stiff and rankling Mr. Prior who, against nature, to her mind, had not come out of his room since taking his silent and hurried breakfast.

"Lord Mercy, my son, you look half in the grave. Do go lay down again now, go on now." But after he'd mumbled out his needs she relented to the extent of a cup of tea and two scones, unbuttered to be sure since it was bad enough to break the mealtime rules at all without being over-fancy about it. "Mind you get back to bed, now, soon's you've finished with that."

I will, Mrs. Grimes, no fear. Perhaps I'll sit out there in the sun-porch for a bit, in the cool."

The tea was having a salutary effect on his outraged system. The scones fell like pacifying lumps.

"Here, why don't you go call your mother now, Eric Croucher? She'd be worried sick if she knew there was something the matter with you."

"Yes, she probably would be, Mrs. Grimes. That's why I don't want to worry her, you see. You know how she is, the bad heart and all."

Mrs. Grimes remembered. Yes, she was always the delicate one, I know. All the Figarys were delicate. And refined, of course, else Harry Croucher wouldn't have picked her and she'd not, after all, made a proper minister's wife. Her own three strapping sons could carry Eric Croucher in one hand. She could do it herself, come to that. No, there was little of his father in that poor white reed, she thought, watching him fade into the wicker rocker in the sunroom. All Olive Figary's doing, that one. Her folk had been bookish, right down the line, teachers and ne'er-do-wells, not like the Grimes, seamen and strong and handy to a man. But she broke off her well-worn reflections when she saw Mr. Morry coming up the gravel pathway to the lodge. Lord knows she had more to do in the kitchen than to let her mind go slipping into these dead old things that had no profit in them.

Mr. Morry pushed through the screen door and said "Oh!" when he saw Croucher and then put his briefcase down tenderly. A go-getter with the firm, Mr. Morry sported tailor-made greys and darker hues, with matching vests and French-cuffed shirts. There was, in his background, the outhouse and years of hand-me-down britches and a brother in an Ontario penitentiary, a predictable fate from which the war years had providentially diverted him, although he preferred to attribute it to an innate sense of self-worth. He sat down, flashing globular gold-plated cuff-links, eyeing Croucher with the assumed air of the man who need not take notice unless he chooses to do so.

"Trouble there, Mr. Croucher? Not feeling too good today?" He clasped his well-kept hands, showing his silvery banded wristwatch and Masonic ring to best advantage. The day had gone well for him, and his self-esteem fattened in contemplation of the semi-collapsed bank clerk.

"Never had one that I can recall," said Mr. Morry of nosebleeds and, by tone, of any other of the fleshly shocks. With disapproval he watched Croucher light up a cigarette. To Mr. Morry physical weaknesses came from wrong thinking, which in turn led to bad habits, which led to so-on and so-on. "I wonder if you've thought about a different line, Mr. Croucher? Not to poke a nose in where it's not wanted, mind you, but I mean, well, cooped up all day in an office, you know. Could be bad, eh, for the old constitution?"

"It's not all bad," Croucher replied defensively. The cigarette tasted raw, the smoke taking on the savour of clotted blood. "There are good opportunities, too."

"Yes, well. But a more active job is what I was implying. Fresh air, outside more, I mean. For a young fellow like yourself, something that doesn't restrict you so much." He himself was feeling very unrestricted at the moment: he was fit, and on the way up; everybody at the firm knew that. "No sense getting into a rut, eh, at your age. What are you now — eighteen, nineteen?"

Croucher was twenty-two. At twenty-two Mr. Morry had already put in three years in the Royal Navy. Discipline, danger, hard refining. Ah well, there had to be book-keepers too he supposed, and something of the condescension he had felt in those wilder days for the steel-haired spectacled clerks in the shore offices came back to him. "My nephew is in for engineering right now. Oh, I can tell you, the outdoor work, you know, built him right up and he used to be, well, something like yourself, Mr. Croucher. No offence mind you, but underweight, so-to-speak."

"Perhaps you're right," Croucher allowed weakly. "Actually, I have been thinking about a more out-of-doors type of work." And so he had been, if one could so consider the mixed wash of western paperbacks he had been reading of late, Riders of the Purple Sage, Last of the Plainsmen.

"Good, good," said Mr. Morry, checking the time on his flashing silver wristwatch. Another problem straightened out or at least the way shown to a possible solution. Now there was the real work of the world to get on with, orders for screws and nails to be written up, a management course to be studied. Croucher sat for a while longer, finishing his smoke, watching a bank of grey clouds form seaward over the mouth of the great bay. Rain was forecast: the sun had already weakened and the wind had turned easterly off the rolling Atlantic. He shivered suddenly and went inside to lay again on the hard, narrow bed, hungry again and with supper still more than an hour off. Listless, he picked up a copy of Riders of the Purple Sage and tried to read the time away, but Mr. Morry had spoiled that escape for him. After a few minutes he fell into a light, fitful sleep from which he was aroused by a burst of loud voices from the sitting-room outside his door. It was a quarter of six, fifteen minutes to table time.

When he came out of his room he found Mr. Morry in heated conversation with Mr. Skimple and the manager, the last two noticeably pink of face and loose of tongue, obviously well primed by their late afternoon stay at Mr. Rump's. Apart from the brief flicker of Mr. Devine's eyelids, his entrance went unacknowledged and, ill-at-ease, he sat down in a stiff, under-stuffed armchair and tried to remain unfelt and unseen, hiding himself behind an ancient copy of the *Evening Telegram*.

"Anyway," continued Mr. Morry, "who is pushing Canada down our throats is what I'd like to know. They say the Water Street gang got their axes to grind, but what about the Confederation bunch? Not in this out of pure love of the land, not by a long shot."

This was directed at Mr. Devine who greeted the sally with a calm and judicious expression on his flushed face. "Oh, let's be charitable, Mr. Morry. After all, all hands are patriotic, I'm sure. Don't you agree, Mr. Skimple?"

Mr. Skimple nodded vigorously. "Certainly it's up to every Newfoundlander to be patriotic in his choice, gentlemen. There may well be powerful voices, the rich and the rich-to-be, shall we say, seeking their own advantage. That's to be expected, after all."

"All right then!" Mr. Morry leaped into the breach. "All patriotic, all wanting the best for the old rock, let's say. Now then, who would be the best to speak up on it, who would be the best to follow? Men who have been successful, like Crosbie, for example? Or my own boss, say? I mean, why not look to them for sound leadership instead of to those others, Bradley and Smallwood and the like, who couldn't even run a pig farm 'twixt the both of them."

"To be fair now, Mr. Morry," protested the manager. "Mr. Bradley is a fine upstanding man in most eyes, a real statesman, if we have anyone worthy of that name, and nothing to do with pigs or the-like as well-you-know."

"All right," conceded Mr. Morry, "I take that back. But do we want a Columnist running the place? And don't tell me Smallwood's not that, or close to it, a Socialist at the least." He looked to Mr. Skimple for support.

"As to that, sir, as far as I know, it's only rumour at best," said Mr. Skimple, "and at any rate, it's a strange enough flower to try and plant in this country, I'm sure."

Mr. Devine, amused almost beyond tact by Mr. Morry's slip-of-the-tongue, took up the chase. "As a banker, Mr. Morry, I'm inclined to let that sort of thing go by the board. I mean, let's look hard at the economics of the thing, that's my concern in the matter, sir."

"Only to say" Mr. Skimple put in, "it's not everything, Mr. Devine, in my opinion. There's the money to worry about, certainly, but my faith, gentlemen, is with the plain Newfoundlander, with the old captains like Bailey and Penny and the like, the delegates close to the sea and the real way of life here. To a man, sir, they are for Responsible Government."

"Yes, and you'll soon see it all down the drain faster than you can think," said Mr. Morry, grateful for this oblique support. "The good-old times, I mean, the honesty and the hospitality and all the rest of it. Out the door it all goes with Confederation."

Mr. Devine cleared his throat: he was uncertain as to the nature, let alone the value, of the so-called good-old ways. They were will-of-the-wisps to his mind, not worthy of consideration in the practical affairs of business and state. "But surely, Mr. Skimple, you can see the advantages of sound finances. And, Mr. Morry, you can't mean the good-old ways will die out just because people are better off. Surely our way of life will survive prosperity, wont it?"

"Well, I can still look to the ones who are against it, Mr. Devine," protested Mr. Morry. "Even the RCs are against it. Even they don't want the French coming here. Archbishop Roche is hard against it, for example: even he doesn't want them Quebecers parlyvousing down here and I'm not the one to fault him on that, I can tell you. I'm a veteran and there's many of us will not forget the frenchies turning against King and Country like they did, sir."

Croucher picked up his ears: it was evident from the drift of the discussion that the manager was being boxed into a tight corner where talk of trade and commerce would avail little against the flood of popular slogans and misconceptions now unleashed by Mr. Morry.

Mr. Skimple now attempted to partially extricate the unhappy Devine. "Mind you, Mr. Morry, I've lived with the French in Quebec. Oh, I even picked up a bit of the language, you know. *Je parle bien la francais,* you know, indeed I speak it well enough when need be." He paused to give his audience time to wonder at this revelation. "Still, while we are British here, as you say, and to me that is worth all the gold in Ottawa — at the same time we can't ignore the finances either. No, it's on a sound business footing we must take back the reins, we can all agree on that."

Mr. Morry was diverted from his attack. "Still, it's a shame." he allowed. "Now I don't lay blame on the Old Country. God knows she's got her plate full right now, but, yes, they'd be happy enough to see our birthright go sailing up the St. Lawrence. I hate to say it, but that's the way it is, gentlemen."

Mr. Skimple rose to take the fly, but before he could speak the kitchen door opened and Mrs. Grimes, aproned and red of face, emerged. "Come on now, gentlemen, there's time enough for your politics. Dinner's ready. Now I wish you'd called a bit earlier, Mr. Devine. It's potluck you'll have to be putting up with." But with supper a half-hour behind schedule Mr. Devine could tell she'd put something special out for them. It was his due, after all: a bank manager was still no minor figure in this neck of the woods.

"Now, now, Mrs. Grimes., you know very well you set the best table in Newfoundland."

"Indeed she does, better than any in the city, Mr. Devine," added Mr. Skimple, moving to the dining room table with obvious keenness of appetite. Mr. Morry, still shaking his head over thoughts of Perfidious Albion, followed the leaders, with Croucher bringing up the rear.

"Oh Lord. I almost forgot him sure," said Mrs. Grimes. She had emerged from the kitchen again, her hands wringing her apron.

Mr. Morry glanced quickly around the table. "Ah yes. And where is Mr. Prior? — the school inspector," he explained to Mr. Devine.

"Well, I'd best go in and see if he's dead or alive," sighed Mrs. Grimes but Mr. Devine held up an arresting hand. "Now don't you be bothering with that, Mrs. Grimes. Here, Eric Croucher. Run in for Mrs. Grimes and see if ... see if he's ready to sit down with us."

Croucher felt his face burn. The nerve of the man, as if they were still in the bank instead of in Croucher's own home, as it were. By God, but wouldn't he be taking Mr. Morry's counsel after all. With an unaccustomed colour in his cheeks he got up and went down the hallway to number three and tapped lightly on the door. "Mr. Prior? Are you up for supper, sir?"

He was putting his knuckles up for a second time when he heard it, a choked mewl, a sob caught in mid-gush from the other side of the door. Surely not, he thought. But yes, there it was again, unmistakably, a muffled anguished crying. Slowly he dropped his hand and stood for a long uncertain moment listening. But the sound was not repeated and finally he unclenched his fist and went back to the dining room.

"He's coming is he?" asked Mrs. Grimes. She had not put a bowl of her famous home soup down in Mr. Prior's place.

"Ah, no." Croucher hesitated. "I guess he's not feeling up to it at the moment, Mrs. Grimes."

"Good Lord," she moaned. "I'd better go in and make sure he's not dying on us."

"Oh, he's after taking a pill, Mrs. Grimes," Croucher said quickly. "To help him sleep, perhaps. But I'm sure he'll be out for the convention broadcast."

"Well, we'll have to leave him be," she said resignedly. The others began to spoon their soup and regain the lost momentum of their interminable discussion.

"I still maintain, sir," said Mr. Skimple, fixing Mr. Morry with his reddened eye, "I still say it will not be Westminster that will sell us up."

Croucher stared at his eye floating in the rich broth amidst the wrecked carrots. He shut his ears to the talk. Surely there could be no doubt that he would leave the bank and set out for that free life under the wide open sky. To Saskatchewan, perhaps, if they brought it about, the Confederation thing with Canada. Yes, had he not heard talk about that, about the vast prairies out there?

# THREE NOTES

*I*t was the tenth anniversary of Marty's death and Wallace Wheeler was in the slough of despond that engulfed him every Mayday. Uneasiness came upon him a week or so before the 24th, intensified as the holiday approached and then subsided fitfully over the next fortnight or so. If he could have managed to do it decently, without giving offence to Tom and Amelia, he would have happily taken his annual vacation every May — go on a trip that would take him out of Corner Brook or, better still, out of Newfoundland altogether.

This was Marty's legacy. This was what he had left behind, others' regrets, others' guilt. A short wasted life, a fierce wild life, a woodland creature, glimpsed from the corner of the eye. Unknown, incomprehensible. The "wild one", that's what Tom and Amelia, bitter and afraid, used to call him. *One of the wild ones,* everyone in town agreed, a wasted life everyone said.

"Are you ready, Wallace?" His mother was calling from the foot of the stairway.

"Just a minute, mother."

He regarded himself again in the dresser mirror. Harris Tweed jacket, subdued, the slightest hint of blue, charcoal grey flannel slacks, black tie, white shirt. Suitable for the occasion. His hair, he noted again, was thinning a bit on the top, but nothing to worry about yet. He was only twenty-nine, after all, and you had to expect to lose a bit as time went by, especially when you worked as hard as he did. Still, perhaps Amelia, with her not-so-subtle hints, was right, and he should be getting married sooner rather than later. He had money enough for it and no one in town had better prospects. He looked regular enough, too, straight nose, lips a bit thin, but good teeth. A girl had once told him he looked like a banker and what was wrong with that?, he had asked himself, puzzled. Had she meant something derogatory? Marty had been the gypsy one — curly-haired, dark-eyed, roguish-looking rogue — function following form. Stray genes, suppressed for a generation or two, one side or the other? How the girls must have loved it, letting him …

He shook his head, frowning at his reflection. What thoughts seemed to crowd in on this day, especially on this day. All the same, she must have meant something derogatory by the observation, as if he had a dollar sign emblazoned on his forehead or something. Well, so be it. In the final analysis, that was what the soul was, after all, whatever it was you wanted most. Money, power, whatever. Art. Poetry. Marty's would have been cobbled together by sex and booze, yet he was beloved for his 'soul'. He'd had "a good soul" someone had said at the wake. No, he'd had a "great soul" someone had said. A great soul. He shook his head again.

Outside it was a mid-spring Wednesday morning, with a touch of winter chill still in the air, the street awash in cold hard sunlight. The brightness helped, though, and Wallace again thanked whatever powers there were that his brother had not died in February or, even worse, in soggy miserable April. The folks were already in the car, looking, as usual, annoyed and stressed. "She sounds rough," Tom complained when Wallace had slid into the front passenger seat. "Does she sound rough to you, Wallace?"

The Nash was brand new and Wallace assured him for the umpteenth time that she was not running rough at all. But Tom Wheeler would worry anyway. For years now he could no longer take joy in what he used to consider the fruits of his life and labour: the wife he still loved, the good son, the thriving business. Instead, a flood of fretfulness seemed to have rushed in as if to fill an empty place inside him that not been there before this had happened, or a place he had never been aware of before. Now if a shingle loosened on the roof he would visualize the whole house slowly crumbling down around their ears. What if (he made up the wildest causes) bunches of people stopped taking medications, or if some doctors, all of them perhaps, stopped prescribing them? Perhaps something bad would happen to Amelia, or perhaps Wallace would marry someone they didn't like, some strange girl they couldn't get along with. Once incipient, chronic anxiety had sharpened in him over the ten years since Marty's death.

"I hope you keep it under fifty when you're out. For the first thousand miles, they told me you should keep it under fifty."

Amelia Wheeler sighed and sat limply in the back seat, taking in the familiar passing scene. They went down West Valley Road and straight into Park Street, heading for the West Side. Marty was buried in Curling, where Tom had been born and raised, in a family plot next to his grandparents. Her own people were from Bonavista Bay, East Coast people, and she was uneasy about ending up underground in Curling. The United Church cemetery was all so rough looking and … what was the word she wanted? Exposed, that was it, so open and unprotected, so impermanent looking. But she would have to be now, of course, if she wanted to be with him. And with Tom and Wallace, of course. There was room for Wallace, too.

She glimpsed the back of the police station as they came to the top of Fisher's Hill. From here the road ran down to the bridge over the brook, the boundary between the West Side and the Townsite. The fleeting glimpse was enough to remind her, to bring back another painful memory, and she sighed, remembering the day Sergeant Harry Burns had come looking for him. "Oh my God, Harry. Is he all right? What did he do?"

It was good of him to come over in his civvies, there were always so many eyes watching and waiting. He was a good friend to them, Harry Burns. But she hadn't let him say a word until she had phoned Tom at the drugstore and made him come home right away. She had steeped tea in the kitchen, leaving the policeman alone in the living room. Perhaps she would make the tea, set out the cups and saucers on a tray, but he would be gone when she took it in. Perhaps he would never have been there. Then Tom had rushed in, tense and frowning, steeling himself for more bad news.

"Marty is in a bit of trouble again, Tom. Seems likely he stole a car over on the West Side last night." Did they know where he was?

At what's-his-name's last night, wasn't he? A bunch of them going to some cabin? Soper's, they thought it was, out on George's Lake. But look, were they sure it was him? Was he sure, was Harry himself sure, that it was Marty?

"Ed Buckle called it in this morning. You know that bright green Studebaker he drives? Stands out like a sore thumb. We found it out on the Stephenville Road a ways, one fender dented in pretty bad." Yes, and Marty had been seen. Two witnesses had seen him actually, and one of them was none other than Constable Art Bugden, strolling up Main Street, and remembering clearly how it seemed a bit queer at the time, seeing Marty driving around in Ed Buckle's "snotty-green Stude."

"I had a chat with Ed." Harry had assured them. "He's a decent chap, Ed, and he'll go along with just having the dent fixed. But he's pretty mad, let me tell you. Tom, Amelia, look, something's got to be done, you know."

Of course, something had to be done. But what?

They were climbing Buckle's Hill and now turning into Broadway, the West Side's untidy commercial roadway. Tom slowed to a crawl, his foot gently tapping the brake peddle, wary of pedestrians who seemed oblivious to the few motorcars that intruded on their space. It was getting to be a heavy day for him as usual, everything, time, the sound of their voices, his stomach, even the air about them, heavy, leaden. It was nearly ten in the morning and the day's spent hours seemed to have piled up like clumps of wet pug behind his eyes. He could feel his heart pump sluggishly.

"Would you take the wheel, Wallace, please?"

"What's wrong?" Amelia cried sharply. Her hand flew to the upholstery behind Tom's right shoulder, the alarm in her voice palpable. He pulled to the curb in front of the Palace Theatre and turned and patted her hand. She tried to clutch his fingers but he was sliding over to the passenger side as Wallace came around to take his place. She was living, he knew, in a cocoon of fear. Marty's death had been like a veil lifted for her, a curtain raised on the uncertain play of her life, of all their lives. "It's nothing, my dear," he reassured her. "Breakfast just sitting there, y'know."

Wallace pulled away from the sidewalk, with a beep of the horn to alert unwary street-crossers. The dreary shopfronts slipped by until they were around the last slight turning at Tommy Coomb's furniture store and making their way up to the Curling road. Tom felt the threat of nausea subside. He should have learned by now that the anniversary meant interior plumbing problems, as sure as night followed day. He ought to have taken something, would have if he'd been thinking straight. After all, he was a pharmacist, he should know better than to have had any breakfast at all. Full gut, guilt, grief. Bad prescription it was.

He looked sourly down the jumbled rocky incline to the mean roofs of Crow Gulch and the slate-blue waters of the bay. How did people live in such awful places he often wondered vaguely, how did the children live? How many didn't? And just off there, in the cold salty estuary, was where Marty had died. Someone, staring out of one of those small dirty windows, might even have seen it happen, watched indifferently perhaps, like someone watching that Greek fellow, what was his name?, falling out of the sky with the burnt wings on him.

"It can't go on," Sergeant Harry Burns had stressed. "He'll be in some real trouble if something's not done. We can keep this one out of the court, but one of these times, Tom …" Breaking into his uncle's cabin, don't forget that one. And the Goodyear and House business. It was a good thing they had had friends in high places on that one. And then he told them, the two of them holding hands on the sofa like scolded schoolchildren, about what Father O'Hara had told him, about the famous Father McIlhenry up at St. FX. "Not one of your common parish fellows."

Harry had assured them. "A Jesuit, McIlhenry, and Father O' Hara says he's got the great reputation for straightening out bent nails."

"I saw Father O'Hara yesterday," Tom said over his shoulder. He had thanked him again, and given him a cheque for a hundred dollars. Every Mayday Tom gave the priest a cheque, even though things hadn't worked out as hoped. Amelia nodded and shrugged. She had always wondered why a Catholic priest would bother about Marty, especially with that bunch of rowdies he had in his own crowd to worry about. "He meant well, I suppose," she said.

Yes, yes, he had meant well, Wallace thought to himself, all of them had meant well. And Marty had gone off to Saint Francis Xavier while he had returned to Dalhousie for his last year, doing all the dry stuff, pharmacology and marketing and the like. And what was Marty studying? Arts, of course. That was to say, nothing. He was in *A Midsummer Night's Dream* that fall, and one of Amelia's favourite photographs, now her most cherished, was Marty as Oberon, with the hair done up and the red rouged cheeks. "He looks so like Errol Flynn," she used to say, and they would tell her yes, so he did, even if they didn't think so. And writing poetry, not too bad either, according to Tom, or from what Tom had been told by the famous Father McIlhenry himself. Well, it was all gone now anyway, as dead as the poet. Probably all cribbed, truth to tell. And then even St. FX had had to let him go, drinking, drunken girls in the dorm and all. Too much in the end, Marty, even for the Jesuits.

Amelia would not look upon the cruel bay waters. She kept her eyes on the northward rockface, remembering how easy it had been with Marty, after the hard time she'd had with Wallace. Happy times too, after, for her, and for Tom too, for all of them, for Wallace too. The happiest time of their lives. Yes, he had turned out wild, but always vulnerable too. If you only knew him you'd see that right off, how vulnerable he was, and never mean, never nasty. It was that crowd he had fallen in with that she blamed, West Side rowdies, Trasks and Powers, Irish and Catholic, and Tommy White, well, not Irish maybe, Lebanese or something, but Catholic all the same, and with too much money to boot. Tommy White with that flashy speedboat …

"Here we are," said Wallace, turning off the roadway.

The church was a woodframe clapboard affair, with a stunted and still-empty bell tower. A row of arched windows, some of them in faux-stained glass, ran down its severe sides, and lilac bushes and wind-tossed flowerbeds softened the weathered façade. It was flanked by a square of graveled parking space and from the front steps there was a view of the wide outer reaches of the Humber Arm. At the back, rising gently inland, was the cemetery.

Too raw, Amelia said to herself again, too open. He should be somewhere under stooped weeping trees, surrounded by mossy old stones, ancient ivy-covered mausoleums, age-tipped crosses. He'd had the real poet's touch, that's what the Jesuit had told Tom, and they were supposed to know about things like that.

> *On daughters' arms old moons are hung,*
> *Old stars trail cobwebs to their sunstruck nests*
> *And O, in the wide wild days when we were young,*
> *Pawns of the moon and the sea's soft tongue.*

That was all she had, all that was left. What had the priest called it, a French thing, vanilla? No, that couldn't be it. She had found it afterwards in a drawer, the only thing left. Marty had discarded the lot, all the paper, Tom said, but he had b1een too distracted, too numb with it all, to take much notice of it. All he remembered was the long excruciating drive, in a cocoon of hurt and anger, across Nova Scotia to the ferry and home.

Wallace unhooked the winter-worn wrought-iron gate, and they made their way to the rectangular family plot. A pitted cement border ran around the waiting spaces, marked for the time being by a simple *Bakelite* plaque set in the centre: MARTIN 1929-1948 BELOVED SON. They had not picked out a proper headstone yet, or decided on inscriptions or the like. Tom wanted a full-length granite one put in, ready to be chiseled as required, with himself to be put down there, to Marty's right, with Amelia there to the left. There was room for Wallace, too, and for a wife if things turned out that way. For grandchildren too, perhaps. His own mother and father were there, a few steps away, and his paternal grandmother too, her stone gathering-in the war-lost grandfather.

Amelia, however, was resisting all his cemetery plans, silently but effectively, and for reasons he could sense if not fully comprehend. Already six years had gone by and her wavering seemed undiminished. She wanted a line from Marty's poem on it, but which one, which one? Or a whole verse, perhaps, but which, which? The words she liked most … *the soul full sail, the wild heart singing* … Reverend Sherren had said that was okay, he didn't see anything wrong with them. But what would people think, being reminded of the wild heart?

Tom and Wallace, what would they think?

"Not too weedy this year," Wallace observed, regretting the remark immediately. Silence was his mode here, the silence of the intruder. He picked a few errant blades of grass, removed a small dandelion, leaving intact the bitter root. Amelia took the wreath she was carrying out of its wrapping — baby's breath, shy lily of the valley, white lilies — passed the tissue and wrapping paper to Tom, and laid it gently on the humble marker. Wallace had brought cushions from the car for the two of them to kneel on.

He relieved Tom of the wreath wrappings and stood mute behind his kneeling parents, trying again to come to some settled understanding of how he felt about Marty. Guilty for sure, but why, he wasn't so sure. True, they had never got along very well, but there had always been a sort of *entente* between them. 'Don't bother me, I won't bother you' sort of thing. And he was three years the elder, too, that had to be kept in mind. Perhaps, just perhaps, it had been more of an injury than he had thought it to be, that one great incident.

Marty had turned up in Halifax in mid spring, sitting there on the front steps of Wallace's boarding house when he came home from university in the evening. Supper first, he'd slipped Mrs. Drucker a few dollars, and then down the road to the tavern for a draft or two. It had been surprisingly exciting and satisfying to have Marty there like that, pleasant to be brothers together in these unfamiliar surroundings, he playing the mellow elder host to the eager youth. Perhaps they saw each other for the first time then and in-the-whole as it were, free to see and hear, not through the eyes and ears of Tom and Amelia, but through their own. How foolish he had been. Marty didn't say he'd been kicked out of

St. FX, of course, and he had gone and spoiled every-thing anyway. Wallace still felt anger when he recalled coming home the next evening and finding Marty three sheets to the wind and his little flat a wreck. The damn fool had grabbed him by the shoulder and tried to dance him about the place, babbling drunkenly. "Lissen, Wallace, lissen. Three notes, Wallace. I'll play 'em again, Wallace, lissen." A borrowed record from the library, pristine and unplayed, Beethoven's something, with Marty chasing the floating needle, scratching it, screech-ing across the spinning vinyl. And on the floor his favorite Sinatra, with a gouge right across the face of it, album jackets and other records in total disarray. Even now a bitter taste rose in the back of his throat when he thought of it. Angrily, he had shoved his drunk of a brother into a night bus, barely able to keep from punching him out on the spot, and the next night, as if it were an afterthought, Amelia had phoned to tell him about the expulsion.

"I wish we could plant a tree, Tom," Amelia was saying. "Do you think they would let us put one there, a willow there, right over the plot?"

Tom was nodding, pleased she was finally taking an interest. "I was thinking the same thing, my dear, the very same thing. Jerry Boland is not so sure about a willow, though, with the water table situation and all that. Maybe something tougher, he says. Crab apple is nice, you know."

Crab apple would be nice, they agreed, very nice, indeed. And wouldn't it have blossoms by *Mayday*, Amelia wondered? Oh, Tom thought it would, yes, he was sure it would. Yes. Look over there, isn't that a crabapple in bloom, right across the road there? And a proper monument, one for all of them, she said.

Granite would be fine. That and the tree over him.

Wallace took her elbow as she got up and gathered up the pillows as she and Tom made their way back to the car. He held them, pausing for a few seconds to contemplate the family burial ground. They would lay on each side of him. It would be their tree, shading them, dappling their pebbly, thinly-grassed plots, petals floating down on them in the spring, Tom and Amelia and Marty. But even as he thought it, he knew he was being silly and irrational.

What would it matter. after all, when it's all over. Still, an angry tide welled up behind his eyes as he put the pillows in the trunk, slammed the cover down, and climbed into the front seat.

Tom had taken a back seat with Amelia, holding her hand, looking almost satisfied at her sudden interest in his long-cherished plans for the family plot. "Keep her under fifty for a bit more, Wallace," he said absent-mindedly as they turned out into the Curling road.

# BRIEF CANDLES

S ure it's not so terrible at all," insisted Cissie Burke. "Not really, Francis, not at all. I mean, I don't think it's nearly as terrible as you said, really I don't."

Mr. Frank Sullivan winced. She would go doubling and tripling on as usual. Supposed, though, to have the grand eye for this sort of thing, that's what they all said about her, the grand eye for art and the like. Very refined, they all said, Cissie Burke was.

"So you think it will do? A shanty in Donegal? The cottage of an Irish peasant? And look how cramped it's going to be too, Cissie. Now don't tell me you don't think it's too cramped."

The lights were off in the Majestic Theatre, except for two or three low footlights along the stage skirting and a single overhead spot that fell bleakly on David Dingwell's foreboding backdrop. A wave of misgivings rolled over Frank as he took in the grim scene. There was no doubt he had been careless in not more closely overseeing the doing of the set, and now here they were, a full dress rehearsal on for tomorrow night, the Bishop himself there with a full pack of Sisters in tow, and half the Fathers to-boot.

"Oh, only a bit, Francis, only a bit," Cissie allowed, squinting into the cavernous semidarkness of the movie house. The place was stuffy and overheated, even for a raw March teatime, and she felt sweaty and uncomfortable under the weight of her winter coat. It was irritating too, him looking so, oh what was the right word, temperate, so neat and tidy as usual, the waxy eyebrows and the neat cut on him as if he'd just stepped out of the barber's chair. To think she had fancied him for a week or so and now only felt like reaching out and mussing up his hairdo. "Oh, it'll do, Francis, I really think it will, really."

He sighed resignedly. She would persist in calling him Francis. "You'll have to watch it, coming in from the right there. And that table. Much too big, much too big." Everything was irritating and disappointing. He had wanted them to tackle *The Playboy* perhaps, *The Countess Cathleen* or the like. Yet here they were, another bit of fluff. Cissie as Molly O'Bannon, sweet colleen of the County Donegal, clever and pretty, managing her rapscallion of a *Da'*, the infamous Seamus O'Bannon, and her dolt of a brother Liam, the two of them the slipperiest poachers in the whole of the West of Ireland. "Don't you ever get fed up with it, Cissie, for heaven's sake? It's all we ever do, year after year, vulgar trash like this. Why not a bit of Yeats, or Synge, some of the great stuff, O'Casey. Something from a real writer. One of the great ones. Irish, of course. Or not even Irish for that matter, Ibsen say, or one of the Russians, say."

Cissie almost laughed out loud. The very idea, something not Irish on St. Patrick's Day. Anyway, it was Father O'Hara who had the last word on the matter and Frank's pleadings for something loftier had simply gone straight into the good man's right ear and straight out the left one. "Sure, I suppose you'll be wanting to put on Shakespeare next," he had chided Frank, good naturedly but with an unmistakable hint of exasperation. Besides, the priest had told Cissie, it seemed he was a barefaced pagan at best, that fellow Yeats. Frank might yearn for the Abbey Theatre sort of nonsense, but what was the worth of it, O'Casey and the like, and hardly a Catholic either, let alone a good one, in the lot of them. It just wouldn't do for here, not in Corner Brook, not in Newfoundland at all for that matter. And the Bishop himself, born and bred a Dubliner, agreed totally, make no mistake there.

"It has that comical bit about the salmon, Francis," Cissie comforted. "That should go over big, don't you think?"

Frank turned from the grim stage to take in Cissie's round pleasant face. Pretty was the right word for her, perky and pretty, and the crowd had loved her in last year's production, especially the men. He was sure too that she had been interested in him earlier, and although she was back to playing the convent girl on him lately, he still planned to bed her. All in good time, if he played his cards right.

"Maybe you're right. Half the crowd will be after jigging a fish now and then, I dare say. Yes, they'll get a laugh or two out of Seamus and Liam, no doubt. But what about your lover, do you think? Do you suppose that bit of business will go over?"

Even in the gloom he could tell she was blushing. "I think it'll be grand, Francis, the way she outsmarts him all the time. And Ozzie is playing him to a *T*, don't you think so? Lord Algernon?"

He did not think so at all. Ozzie Walsh was a big pain-in-the-neck as far as he was concerned, with that foolish accent, as phony as a three-dollar bill, something he's caught out of a George Formby picture show no doubt. Wouldn't be corrected, of course, wouldn't be guided in the matter at all. Lord Algernon speaking Cockney ... what a farce! Still, she had it right about one thing. Ozzie was a true clown, and the crowd would love watching him fumble and bumble, outfoxed time after time by a little Irish wisp of a thing, and then losing his heart to her in the bargain.

He glanced at his watch. A quarter-to already, and supper was always on the table by six at Mrs. Coleman's. A pleasant enough boarding place it had turned out to be, and the town itself wasn't half bad either. Even so, he missed the city. There was so much more theatre and the like in St. John's, some room to try out new things. *The Playboy* had gone over pretty well three Marches back, at least in his opinion it had. Ned Parsons had complained about the low take, but that was only to be expected. Real theatre that had been, and he had urged them to do something worthwhile again the next year, but to no avail of course. Disappointing it had been, but no surprise when someone else was asked to do the next show, *The Mad Muldoons of Morne*. His transfer to Corner Brook couldn't have come at a better time.

"Will all hands be making it tonight?"

Cissie nodded, glancing at her own wrist. Everybody had been gotten hold of and had promised to show up. "My, just look at the time, will you? I'll see you about seven then, Francis? I told them about seven."

Frank ate supper alone. His fellow boarder, Sergeant Short of the Constabulary, was on the night shift, and his plate was heaped with an extra portion of Mrs. Coleman's Wednesday night Jiggs dinner. He had barely a half hour to wash up and change before setting out to walk to Cissie's, 'cabbage and pease' pudding coexisting heavily in his full stomach.

By seven-thirty the cast and company were gathered at the Burke home on Main Street. David Dingwell was there too, he of the somber backdrop, wearing a mauve kerchief about his scrawny neck, the sight of which made Frank glad he had chosen to put on a turtleneck.

Marion Gregory, who played the saucy village widow Morgan O' Malley, and Barb McGrath, the open-mouthed dim-witted servant girl Biddy Cullen, were side-by-side on the front parlor settee, sweet sherries in hand. Bart Collins, the infamous Seamus O'Bannon, and the unintentionally hilarious son Liam, Gerry Prince, were leaning against the fireplace mantle, Gerry puffing on a cigarette in the furiously nervous way he had about him, Bart, older and a veteran of the local stage, left hand in jacket pocket, relaxed and at ease, a glass of ale in his right. Between them, his back to Frank, stood Martin Bergeron, the perplexed magistrate in the play, talking a blue streak as usual with the hands flying about in all directions. The rest of the cast, nameless peasants, Reg Coombs and John Mullins, and the two hapless Guardia, Billy Lee (Constable Moyle) and Freddy Reddy (Constable Boyle), stood here and there about the large front room. Four or five cobbleseat chairs had been pressed into service, but stood empty around the periphery.

Cissie came bursting in from the kitchen area. What a splendid Pegreen Mike she would have made, Frank couldn't help thinking. The red tint of her hair was just right, with the blue-green eyes and pout of a mouth, the pug nose and high cheekbones. She had the voice for it too, carried clear as a bell it did, none of the screeching and straining most of them had to make of it. Play it to perfection she could, with every man in the audience sucking a back tooth at the sight of her.

"What will you have, Francis? Sherry? There's a bit of port, I think, and lots of beer."

He'd have a spot of sherry please, dry stuff if she had it, Mrs. Coleman's pudding demanding something a bit sharp to keep it mollified. He watched her swinging return to the kitchen, the hips so slim and boyish under her clinging calf-length skirt. What was that? About the table? Freddy Reddy was tugging at his sleeve.

" … way too big, Frank, we were thinking. Weren't we, Bart? We stopped by the Majestic this afternoon …"

"Yes, in Act Three there, Frank. You know … where the salmon is being tossed out the window? If the thing gets dropped … well … the whole thing will just fall to pieces, won't it?"

What did they think, that he was directing the thing but hadn't bothered to read it? Of course it mustn't be dropped, the audience having been led to believe the bundle was the Widow O'Malley's babe-in-arms. Any idiot could see that the Magistrate's consternation and Lord Algernon's bewilderment, all would be for naught, if they dropped the stupid thing. And hadn't he said as much to Cissie Burke just two hours past, about the table being too wide?

He held out his palms as if to mollify an unruly classroom. "I'm sure we can come up with something better, Freddy. I'll call Dick Peddle in the morning…"

"You can use the one out here in the kitchen," Cissie called out.

Except it was all chrome, objected Bart. "Would you find the like of that in Donegal? Back then, I mean."

Oh yes, it just had to be wood, insisted Marion, and oh yes, sure it just had to be, agreed Barb. Unless you could put a cloth over it, perhaps, right down to the floor, Marion compromised, and, well, some thought that might be acceptable, others that it still wouldn't do. They would go on and on all night about it, about tables and table cloths and table sizes and table legs, so Frank held up his hand and assured them Dick would certainly know how to fix the problem. "And any other problems, then? With the set, I mean?".

Bart thought having the Sacred Heart hanging on the wall might not be quite suitable, the whole thing being a farce after all. Or even the crucifix for that matter, added Freddy, although he allowed the people involved would obviously be Catholics. Except for the Magistrate, of course. "And Lord Algernon, don't forget," Cissie put in. And then Freddy just had to say it: "Frank, does the back of the thing have to be so grim looking? It's all grey and black and really weird looking, don't you think?"

All eyes, some hostile, most embarrassed, turned to take in the thin mauve-scarfed figure of David Dingwell, who sat sipping tea, cup and saucer balanced on a well-creased kneecap. "Well, I was trying for something a little bit different, you know, something from the modern stage ..."

A chorus of pretended approbation followed. "Yes, yes!" "Very interesting, David, very good ..." "Wake them up for sure, David, that will ..." "Really modern, David, so it is ..."

Encouraged, the artist put aside his cup and saucer. "Actually, I was inspired, you might say, by that little book you loaned me about the Abbey Theatre, Frank. That backdrop for *Riders to the Sea* that's in there? Do you remember the picture that's in there?"

"Ah yes," murmured Frank, feeling tarred now, "thank you very much David," with the same brush. "A good idea, David, I'm sure it will work out just fine, just fine." God, what an idiot. *Riders* indeed, tied into this piece of junk! Better to change the subject, he decided, before they made an even deeper pit out of it. "Anyway, the play's the thing, after all. Any problems with the script at all? I must say, everybody seems to have their parts down pretty well. Except ..."

"And where's Ozzie?" wondered Marion. "Yes, where's the leading man at all?" echoed Barb.

Lord Algernon had not yet made an appearance. A bit foolish, they all agreed, to be going over the thing without Ozzie there, although as far as Frank was concerned it was also a bit of a relief. And typical of Ozzie it was not to show up for the fine tuning, a bit of final polishing.

"Of course I told him," said Cissie, reacting to Frank's raised eyebrow. "I talked to him at the store about five o'clock, just before I met you at the Majestic."

"Better start calling the taverns," Freddy Reddy suggested. Laughter all around. He was the wild one they reminded each other, that Ozzie was, always up to something. Irresponsible bastard Frank wanted to add, but held his peace. Why oh why had he ever given the fellow the lead role in the first place? Whose idea had that been, actually? Cissie's? The high colour in her cheeks and the nervous way she kept looking at her wristwatch jogged his memory. Her it had been, talking him into it. No wonder she looked guilty.

Here it was, nearly eight already. Soon they would all be checking their timepieces. The National Convention broadcast would be on at nine-thirty and hadn't they heard about Joey and Peter going at each other 'hammer and tongs' that very afternoon. Real drama that was, real life drama, the fate of the country hotly debated, no holds barred, no prisoners taken, champions of competing causes chaffing in the lists, the clash of inflamed oratory, this one for Independence, this one for union with Canada, another for hitching up with the United States. "The Newfoundland National Theatre," a wag on VOWN had tagged it, adding that it was hard to tell if it was comedy they were putting on or tragedy.

"Oh well," Bart said reassuringly, "sure, even if he didn't have it down pat, the crowd would still love it, and wouldn't hold a missed line or two against him, he had such a comical touch." Some had thought he should be playing Liam instead, but Frank had had the last word. Ozzie didn't look right for a Liam, he insisted, too tall, too Hollywoodish for it. No, the part of the aristocrat, even such a simple-headed bumbler like Lord Agernon of Aroon, suited him better. Cissie had been right in that, give the devil her due. If only the fellow could come up with a reasonable accent.

"Frank, in the last act there," Martin began, "when I give up on the whole thing and just throw the case out of court, could we get a few more hands onto the stage do you suppose? Rig up a few more chairs?"

Martin had it right, Frank agreed, it would certainly add a more lively air to the proceedings. But, he pointed out again — wondering if Martin Bergeron ever listened to anything anybody said to him — there would have to be costumes, and where would they stand, or sit, given the way the stage was, and when would they cheer, or groan or whatever and so on. And to carry Seamus off on their shoulders, as someone else had suggested, would require a team of lumberjacks, considering Bart's girth. Oh far too much business in it, he explained again, far too much business.

Freddy, as might be expected, picked up the standard and pressed on. "It's the author himself who suggests it, Frank, right here on page 38: *An alternative not be overlooked as a means of heightening the astonishment and joy engendered by the Magistrate's outrageous ruling.*

"Yes, Freddy, I know. But it's only a suggestion,

Freddy. only a suggestion." He could no longer keep the annoyance from showing, try as he might. For God's sake, did the fellow think he'd never set eyes on page bloody 38? "And we had all this out about a month ago, Freddy, don't you remember? There was trouble enough getting the cast together as it was, let alone half a dozen more. And anyway, with the way the stage is, with all hands coming in from … well, you know."

Eleven sets of eyes carefully avoided looking at David Dingwell, and a chorus of reassurances began. "There'll be a good fuss, don't you worry!"; "The crowd won't notice it a bit, not a bit." And if there was any blame to be laid, Frank could see it plain as day on their faces, it would fall on him not on David. David's first stage job, after all, and if somebody had taken the interest he should have taken … "It's after all that fuss," came Cissie to the rescue, "after the crowd is gone that bothers me, Francis. I mean, it's so hard to believe, isn't it, that Lord Algernon is really head over heels about Molly. I mean, she's done nothing but pull the wool over his eyes the whole night long."

"Ah well," Marion said archly, "stranger things have happened than that, my dear, when it comes to love."

"Or S-E-X," added Billy Lee, and had them all smirking knowingly and nodding agreement.

"Indeed," said Frank, seizing the opening, and admiring the marvelous blush that was blooming on Cissie's lovely cheeks, "it's certainly a bit far-fetched all right. But look, it's not a great play or anything, is it? I mean, we can't take it too seriously now, can we? Considering the isolation of the place, the loneliness of the young squire …"

Cissie sprang from her chair when the front-door chimes sounded. "There, that'll be Ozzie," she cried, rushing out into the front hall. They heard the front door open and then the porch door slam shut, the stamping of feet, a laugh, a squeal of "Ozzie!" from Cissie, and then there they were, the center of the stage, Cissie and Ozzie, Molly and Lord Algernon, each with an arm out thrown to the gathering, each with an arm about the other's waist.

He's drunk, Frank saw immediately, tipsy at best. Oh the trials of the amateur director, the director of amateurs. Egging him on, too, Cissie was, with the silly posturing and carrying-on. Yes, empty-headed she was for certain, innocent perhaps, but empty-headed.

The whole business consumed five or six minutes before Ozzie was finally settled down, sprawling expansively where no other male had dared go, sitting himself between Marion and Bard on the settee. "So what's the topic, then," he demanded, hugging his delighted neighbours. Oh, even Frank had to admit it, the fellow could certainly animate a scene when he wanted to.

"We were talking about the end of it," Martin told him. "Cissie thinks old Algy there wouldn't fall for a simple girl from the barrens like herself."

"No, no," Cissie protested. "All I mean is I don't think there's enough in the first two acts to support it, not nearly enough at all. It comes as such a surprise, all at the end, all so sudden."

"I agree with Cissie," Frank said quickly, holding up a hand to reclaim their attention. Almost eight-thirty already, and he could hardly expect to keep them much longer. "But, as I said, it's such a weak thing, Cissie, you just have to bear that in mind. This writer, Farlen Meara, not one of the leading Irish playwrights, you know. In fact, I think he's actually a Yank, isn't he? So we just have to put up with that sort of thing, because a farce is a farce, after all. I think we could have done better, should have had a better thing to do, something more classic, if you like." He leaned back, putting his elbow on the cover of the upright piano. "And we should keep in mind that there is a tradition in the theatre regarding farce …"

"Yes, yes," Ozzie Walsh boomed in. "Something more classic, Frank, more classic, my son. That's exactly what I was saying myself just the other day, wasn't I, Cissie? What was it you wanted to do? Frank? *The Cuntess from Catalina*, was it, by what was his name, Billy Yeast, was it? Or Keest? And was he the same fellow? Frank, could you tell me now, who wrote that *Ode To A Greasy Peepot* thing, I wonder?"

Squeals and playful slaps from Marion and Barb, and smirks all around. They couldn't help but be amused, or pretend to be. Ozzie was such a clown, although feeling a bit uncomfortable at the same time for Frank, who was upright now, stiff grimace of a smile on his flushed face. "Even a farce has to be taken seriously," he began, but of course no one was listening. Cissie, he saw, was wagging a finger at her naughty Algy, but smiling too.

"Listen, Frank," said Reg Coombs, anxiously eyeing his wristwatch, "I'd really like to catch the Convention tonight, if you don't mind." Others quickly joined in the plea. "Me too, Frank." "Cashin and Smallwood went at it I hear …" "Oh, hammer and tongs boy, hammer and tongs …" "It's almost nine now, Frank." And of all people, David Dingwell crossed the room to lay a timid hand on Frank's forearm, patting his arm actually. "Don't worry, Frank, don't worry. It'll be good tomorrow night, I'm sure it will be."

Frank jerked his arm away. Most of the crew had

already gone out the front door, not waiting for whatever point he had wanted to raise, the most important point, damn it all. A farce had to be done seriously, done just right if you wanted the crowd to go along with it.

Cissie had hold of his arm now. "Oh, David is right, Francis, really he is, really." She took both their elbows, guiding them to the front door. "And don't worry about Ozzie. I'll see to it he's got the lines down just perfect before he leaves here tonight. Don't you worry, Francis, down just perfect."

Frank found himself in the front porch, struggling into his overcoat, hearing over his shoulder Ozzie Walsh wondering if his darling Molly might have a spare ale for her poor thirsty Algy. "In the fridge, Ozzie," she called back to him, "in the fridge." He felt a slight shove between his shoulder blades and stepped out onto the front steps. A light, ethereal snowfall had started. Cissie gave his hand a parting squeeze. "Don't worry so much, Francis. It's all a bit of fun, sure, just a bit of fun."

There was nothing for it now, he knew, walking heavily along Main Street. A bloody disaster, another year wasted, another opportunity missed. The pride he had felt, the surge of gratification when they had asked him to be the director, had proven as ephemeral as a cloud of steam from the paper mill. He had been a fool to take it on, with his soul wandering up among the stars and not the slightest bit at home in the wilds of Donegal, with all its rough and rustic goings-on. Nor in the wilds of Western Newfoundland either, for that matter, let alone the West of Ireland. And his mind was certainly made up, certainly now after this night's doings. Yes, he would most certainly be leaving the damn island altogether now, quitting this land of Philistines forever. Oh, they were all of them that, even Cissie Burke. Yes, especially Cissie Burke, especially that one. Pegreen Mike in the flesh.

Well, but what could you expect, to be raised and schooled in a place like this, where the Bishop could blather on and on about how Athens, the Athens of Ancient Greece, had not been a whole lot bigger than the town of Corner Brook, perhaps not as big. Yes, bigger than Athens, that Athens, big enough to have its own Aristotle if it wanted to — Frank could hardly believe his ears listening to the man — its own Plato or Sophocles or Euripides, if it wanted it badly enough. And then wouldn't stand for having a bit of O'Casey or Yeats in the parish hall.

"Hypocrites!" he hissed into the snowy night.

"What's that?" asked David Dingwell. Frank had forgotten the other, trotting along half a step behind him. "You mustn't take it all so seriously, Frank. They mean well enough, you know, the most of them."

Frank shrugged and sniffed. How could he even attempt to explain things to this underdone little bookworm, this thin reed of a bayman? It was bad enough in St. John's, having to put up with the crowd in there, but out here, out in the Wild West, it was just too much. "Putting on a play is hard work, my friend," he said with condescending bitterness, finishing off with his favourite epigram. "And no play at all for those putting it on."

"Oh, I agree, I totally agree, Frank," persisted the annoying one. "I didn't mean that you didn't have to take it seriously. As the director, yes, of course you have to hold it all together and all that sort of thing. And you're doing a good job of it, Frank, you really are. I just meant, you know, back there, Ozzie acting like that and Cissie. Fooling around ..."

Fooling around? What did he mean?

"Well, you saw them yourself, Frank. I mean, they should keep it to themselves, I think, when it comes to the play and all."

A smattering out of Synge came suddenly into Frank's memory … *If it's a poor thing to be lonesome, it's worse maybe, to go mixing with the fools of the earth.* Phil Vardy had played the lead in St. John's but had never caught the part right, doing Christy as just another one of the dozens of country bumpkins he had played year after tiresome year. But it had still been worth the while, a great thing to have tried, no matter what they had said. *Fools of the earth.* And lonely enough he was, away from the city, not to be in whatever great city it was he belonged in, his unrealized great city.

Escape he must. He belonged to the real theatre world. Of that he had never been so sure. New York, London, Dublin. Local boy makes good in Dublin. *Francis Sullivan of The Abbey.* Or should he aim for New York, go down and look him up in New York, what was his name? Murray? No, Anderson. That was it, John Murray Anderson. Wasn't he still big, down in New York City, John Murray Anderson?

They had come to the corner of West and Main, pausing under the streetlamp at the Bank of Montreal building, facing the modest war memorial across the roadway. David Dingwell would carry on to the West Side, crossing the bridge into an anarchy of crooked streets, jumbled housing and false-fronted shops, while Frank would bear left into the orderly geometric calm of the Townsite.

"Frank?"

He stopped and looked back. The other stood, hands clasped at his waist as if in prayer, bareheaded in the thin snow that was fast turning into a sharp sleet. "About the backdrop and all that. The set. It's not what you wanted, is it? The window's all wrong …" The voice trailed off.

Frank felt a wave of pity, but a contemptuous pity. There was no staging in the world that could redeem the thing, nothing in the whole wide world that could ever redeem it, that could justify its mere existence. Didn't the fellow realize that? Couldn't he see beyond the end of his own nose, for God's sake, couldn't any of them? He should never have loaned him that book on the Irish National Theatre, putting such grand ideas into that poor noggin.

"David, it's a grand piece of work you've done. It'll have them talking for a month. It's too damn good for them to tell the truth."

The artist stood nodding his head, his expression wavering between consolation and uncertainty. Frank almost reached out and patted him on the head.

"Right out of the *Riders*, was it? Inspired, David, inspired that was."

A pause. David stood nodding, a dog waiting for another bone, then turning away with a weak wave of farewell and resignation. Frank watched then cleared his throat and called after the departing figure. "David? What you said about Cissie and Ozzie Walsh … do you know that for certain then?"

The other nodded emphatically. "Oh yes. Everybody is saying it sure. Freddy and Reg and the rest of them. Well, I mean, you saw them just then…"

True enough, he had seen them with his very own eyes. Or rather, he was just now seeing them, watching a scene that had failed to register the first time around. He nodded a final good night and began trudging down West Street towards Mrs. Coleman's. There would be no benefit, especially for him, to start brooding on love's bitter mysteries. No love in it anyway, not a bit of it, in what he had been feeling for Cissie Burke. Nothing to betray, nothing to be betrayed. Damnation on the fellow all the same. Usurper. On the both of them, for that matter. Clown and shrew.

John Murray Anderson. That was something to start thinking about. A letter to prepare the way? To what address, though? What was he running down there? A school? An Agency? First thing, then, a letter, to get an address for *the* letter. But to whom? Or should he just show up in New York City, bold as you please, throwing himself on the great one's mercy? The sort of thing they'd do in a movie. *Carpe diem.* Yes, he must. Faint heart won neither lady nor fame.

Anxiety fluttered familiarly at the edge of resolve. A letter would be only prudent, after all. A courtesy from one St. John's man to another.

*Dear Fellow Newfoundlander?* Perhaps.

# CASUALTIES

O h. I just love this one," enthused Edie Rowe, finger hunting with a furious squint through her program. "Oh, what's that one again, Ralph?"

Ralph Rowe sighed. She was as shortsighted as Mr. McGoo, but wear spectacles? Never in your life. Tried them once but they made her look too old she complained, like she was ready for the nursing home for heaven's sake. Almost twenty-seven, but that was how childish she was, that was Edie.

"Right there," he whispered, jabbing her program. "It's that one there, Edie, *Woman is Fickle*."

As he had feared, she began humming. *Dum dum de dum de dum, dum dum de dum de dum.* "Sssh!" he hissed, "sssh!" but not even the Church Lads Brigade Band at its brassiest could drown Edie's persistent drone. The number of times he'd had to hush her lately, in the movies, at Evensong, was getting downright embarrassing and he was dreading more and more having to go out with her at all.

Lieut. Godfrey was into the *Kashmiri Love Song*, Marilyn Butt on the piano, and very nice it was, too, although Ralph was really waiting for the more stirring numbers, *Colonel Bogey, Sons of the Brave, Our Blue Jackets*, the sort of rousers that got the blood going, gave a fellow a lift of spirits, a surge of patriotism. Still, it was touching, sentimental of course, but touching all the same. All part of the Empire, after all, both sides of the same coin, *Colonel Bogey, arrump-a-thump-thump-thump*, and at the same time 'pale hands loved' and all, tropical incense in the air, perfumes of exotic flowers, dusky-skinned maidens ... *beside-ah thee Shally-*

*mar-ah*. What would that be like, he wondered, dusky maidens, love, fragrant warm flowing waters beside …

A night like this made a fellow proud to have been part of a true blue outfit like the Church Lads Brigade. Mr. Montague Lewin, the paper mill boss, had opened the concert with a little talk about the Brigade, reminding them that the Newfoundland company had been the very first to be organized in the overseas Empire. "How very fitting," Monty Lewin had said, "how very fitting, the first colony, the first overseas Brigade." And what a litany he had made of the grand men who had served and fostered the corps, here in Corner Brook, in St. John's, all over the island, Phelps, Owen Jones, Major Rendell. Professor George Rowe, another great one there, perhaps even a relative somewhere in the tangled past. Even if he wasn't, it was still something to be proud of, just having the family name associated with such a grand enterprise.

*Soldiers Of The King* sang Lieut. Godfrey and, ah now, that's more like it, thought Ralph, his right foot tapping to the beat. Around him the men were straightening up, marking time with heel and knee, toes pressed to the floorboards. Great War veterans a lot of them, and there were some from this one, like George Caines two rows ahead, out of it now with the left leg all shot up. Lucky he was, to be out of it alive, but lucky too, in Ralph's opinion, to have been in it at all. A scattering of uniforms here and there, two or three American, some Canadian navy. Smart looking, the Yank outfits, you had to grant that. There was enthusiastic applause as the lieutenant took his bows. Strapping fellow, looking every bit the part in his smart navy blues, the cut of him a reassurance that the battle was in safe hands. No weak chest there,

Ralph thought ruefully. Sound Mind in a Sound Body. His school motto that had been.

*Dum dum de dum de dum.* Edie was gently swaying now, savouring her new favourite. What had it been the last time? Oh yes, *Come, Come, I Love You Truly*, that was the one. Nelson Eddy, Jeanette McDonald movie. Nearly drove him crazy with that one, he sighed and looked away, resigned, and saw Olive Penney looking at Edie. When he caught her eye Olive changed expression in a flash, but you couldn't mistake the concern in her face. There was no doubt about it, he'd have to sit Edie down and talk to her about the way she carried on in public sometimes. Friends like Olive were starting to show concern, too, and it wasn't just a private thing anymore, something just between the two of them.

He looked around the hall again, trying to spot Margy and her Yankee boyfriend, Marsynzky or Morsinski, however you spelled it, USAF chap from Stephenville. Nice enough fellow, Gene what's-his-name, and well educated according to Margy, although that was surprising considering he wasn't even an officer. When they got home, the kettle would be ready, sandwiches and cake set out on the kitchen table, and Ralph would be feeling uncomfortable knowing she'd been upstairs with her American.

The band was in full flight now, *El Abanico*, loud enough, thank God for small mercies, to drown out Edie's humming. He relaxed a little. Outside he might have put an arm about her, held her from swaying, distracted her somehow. Here inside the hall he would feel awkward doing anything like that, anything drawing attention to them. Should he take hold of her hand perhaps? Anyway, there was only the Whistle Band with a few tunes to go and then *The Banks of Newfoundland* and *God Save The King* to finish off the evening. Margy wouldn't be showing up now, that was for sure.

The Whistles were done — *A Life on The Ocean Wave, We Won't Go Home 'til Morning, The British Grenadiers* — and then, as the last strands of the Banks were fading, they stood for the anthem. A splendid night, all in all, and even Edie had returned, something perhaps in the high pitch of the tin whistles catching her fancy, bringing her back to the present. Funny, he thought, how such a thin sort of music, primitive almost, could have so much power to it. His blood had been stirred by it more than by *Colonel Bogey* played by the whole kit-and-caboodle. Edie's easy soprano rang out pleasingly in *God Save The King*, and he was easily persuaded again that he was imagining things. After all, she was known to be a 'character' his Edie, a "real character," as Margy kept saying.

Lloyd and Olive Penney caught up with them for the walk home along West Street. The low clouds had passed over; the air was pleasant and sweet, washed clean by the light rainfall, the breeze turned about and blowing westerly now over the warm waters of the gulf. Polished stars blazed in the western sky. The two men took the lead, Edie and Olive following, with Edie chatting away and laughing easily with her best friend. Ah, she was all right, Ralph told himself, of course she was.

"The very best, the CLB band," said Ralph, "and I've never heard them better than they were tonight." He hummed a bar or two of *Colonel Bogey*, his rolled up program keeping the beat on his lefthand palm.

"The best of them all," agreed Lloyd.

"The CCC lot couldn't hold a candle to them, not a candle."

"Not a candle," agreed Lloyd again.

Ralph had gone to school with Lloyd, who now had a metal plate set in his left temple, the result of a shrapnel hit "over there." He had been in a coma for three whole months and now he was home, out of the navy, and back at his old job in the paper mill. What had that been like, Ralph often wondered, everything all black and blank for so long? Lloyd had told him he hadn't had a single dream that he could remember, not one in the whole three months.

"Would you slow down a bit, Ralph," Edie called to him. "I told Margy ten-thirty and it's not even 'quarter to' yet."

So Margy really hadn't meant to come at all. He should have known he supposed, but what was the point in not telling him right up front? Why waste the ticket money? Not easy to swallow, either, that she would not only deceive him but then go and rope Edie into the game too. He turned in time to see Edie whispering in Olive's ear, and he could guess what she was saying, the way the two of them were giggling.

"Oh, come on, Ralph, let them have their bit of fun, for God's sake." Edie had taken Lloyd's place and now poked her husband gently in the ribs. "She's a big girl now, you know."

She was right, of course, Margy wasn't his little sister now. She was all grown up and then some, after three years in St. John's and another two at a cottage hospital on the South Coast. Still, an ingrained protective impulse, ineffective and unwanted, persisted. He had even, after overcoming Edie's misgivings, persuaded her to move in with them instead of with their parents in the little house over on the West Side. So much closer to the hospital was the reason they both adopted, although they both knew she'd never be able to stand living with the old folks now.

"He's such a nice guy," Edie was going on, "and I think he's really in love with her, too. You're going to hold what he said that night against him forever, are you? It was all just a joke, you know, the two of them were just fooling around."

They were having a few drinks, a Saturday night get-together, Margy showing off her latest to Lloyd and Olive and a couple of fellow nurses. He had probably been the soberest one in the crowd and he remembered sharply what her new Yank, adopting a condescending stage accent, had said about the "Hempire, old gel, the Hempire begad," and all the rest of it, the sun slowly sinking on it and all that. They hadn't known he'd overheard them out on the back porch and he'd kept his mouth shut for Margy's sake. What would a fellow like that understand about it anyway? — but the intense surge of anger he had felt had been real enough.

Silent, they passed the Public School, closed for the summer, where they had all finished their grade elevens, sound minds in sound bodies. Well, Lloyd anyway, or used to be, and Olive. Edie? At the Humber Pharmacy he turned to ask Lloyd and Olive in for tea and sandwiches, but Olive shook her head. "Not tonight, Ralph. His nibs here is on the midnight shift. Did you tell him you were coming up to the house, Edie?"

She hadn't, of course. He wanted to object because it would leave him to deal with Margy and her visitor all by himself, but there it was, plans for the Saturday night church supper had to be all wrapped up, they had a million-and-one things to decide on. She was sure she had mentioned it to him and anyway she'd be home before midnight at the latest. In fact Lloyd could even see her home, perhaps, on his way down to the mill. Resigned, he walked with them as far as the USO building, said his good nights to Lloyd and Olive and watched the trio cross West Street and begin their chattering stroll across the green towards Central Avenue. Turning, he went into the rear yard of the house on Park Street where Edie had been born and raised and was almost to the back steps before he caught the glow of Margy's cigarette. She was sitting alone on the back porch and he had the fleeting and discomforting feeling she had been watching them. Judging them perhaps, or judging him really.

"Margy? So where's Gene then?"

She waved a hand dismissively, tracing a slow red scratch in the dark. "He was called back to base early. I see Edie is off for a bit."

"Well, you know what she's like. Like sisters, those two, her and Olive."

Margy puffed on her Lucky Strike and leaned over to plump up a cushion on the wicker settee across from her. "Sit down for a bit, Ralph. There won't be too many more nights like this to sit out in. I'll go get you a cup of tea."

She was right about the weather. They could sit out comfortably tonight and enjoy the smells and sounds of late summer, although the air, heavy with the damp breath of dying flowers, was still a bit cool and he should probably be wearing a sweater. She came out with a tray bearing a small pot and a single cup and saucer, and set it down on a low glass-topped table, the steeping tea fragrant in the night air.

"Aren't you having some?"

"Still got a drink down here somewhere," she

said, groping by the side of the settee. Bourbon again, he supposed, and a bit too much of it lately in his opinion. Jack Daniels and Lucky Strikes — Gene's burnt offerings. A drop of scotch now and then was his own limit, and with the weak chest smoking cigarettes was out of the question. She found her tumbler and settled back, lighting up another Strike and draining the whiskey in a single gulp. "Actually, I'm glad Edie's not here for a bit, Ralph. There's something I wanted to talk to you about."

He watched her shadowed face over the rim of the teacup. What you would call striking, Margy was, handsome perhaps, with straight, strong features. An able woman you'd think right off the bat, one to be put in charge of whatever women usually took charge of, and she would likely be the new matron when Nurse Whelan retired next year. It was no wonder her Yank was attracted to her, good looks and a good head on her in the bargain.

"Doctor Bowman is in town next week, Ralph. Remember me telling you about him? From Halifax?"

He felt his chest contract and a familiar uneasy constriction at the back of his throat. This was the specialist that Margy had been enthusing about, an expert, according to her, in all sorts of nervous disorders and the like. The Government paid him to make a railway tour on the island every second year or so, updating the local GPs and doing diagnostic work on referral cases, and she thought Edie should really have a good talk with him. His schedule in Corner Brook was pretty tight, but Margy was sure she could arrange things for her.

"I don't know. I mean, you saw her just now. One hundred percent, wasn't she?"

"Right now, yes, at this very moment, but you know how she's forgetting things all the time, Ralph. Yesterday morning, I swear to God, she came out of the kitchen and asked me if I wanted some breakfast. She had just made scrambled eggs for me, Ralph, not half an hour gone by. And now she's started with this swaying thing too, Ralph, you must notice it. Even Gene noticed it the other night at the movie."

He had to admit it, nod his head sadly to acknowledge the problem. It couldn't be overlooked or covered up any longer. Just think of the way Olive Penney had been sizing her up not an hour ago, the way she'd swayed and hummed right through *Colonel Bogey*. "I think she's waltzing," he sighed. "In her head, you know, waltzing."

Sure it might not be anything serious at all, Margy supposed comfortingly. Something passing, only temporary. Such hard monthlies she had, didn't she? Something to do with that perhaps, hormones or whatever. And not being able to have children, as they had found out, it could all be connected somehow. Dr. Bowman would have seen dozens of such cases, she was certain, and probably would know what to do, what to tell them.

"She's not aware of it herself, at least as far as I can tell." Ralph sipped his tea but it was cold now and too strong for his taste anyway. "The first time she did that swaying thing was at Evensong, about three or four months back. Thank God there wasn't much of a crowd, but even so I think Reverend Loder noticed it. Old Mrs. Cull was behind us and the poor thing looked half scared to death. I'm sure she thought Edie was drunk. But when I tried to talk to her afterwards she wouldn't believe a word of it.

Never such a thing, you know, never. She won't even admit her eyes are gone a bit weak, for heaven's sake, let alone whatever this is."

"How about if I talk to her, Ralph?"

He shrugged. "I don't expect she'll believe it from you, either. As I say, I don't think she knows there's anything odd going on at all."

Margy shook her head, "But she does. Oh yes, she really does, Ralph. When I said, 'Edie I just finished having breakfast sure' there was such a look in her eyes, She's afraid, Ralph. She wants help but she's too frightened to look for it. She's a lot like her mother, remember?"

That could be true, he had to agree, true that she seemed to have that trait in her, as her mother had famously had. Mrs. Manuel had died still convinced her little kidney pills were keeping her on the road to recovery, and it wasn't so much a urinary tract infection that had killed her, according to Margy, as it was her unwillingness to come to terms with facts. And Edie was doing that same thing right now, waltzing herself out of reality. Yes, Margy would talk to her, they decided or, better still, she would have a chat with Olive and together the two of them should be able to persuade her into seeing the great Bowman. Likely it was only something simple after all, the lack of some vitamin or other, some mineral missing perhaps, something like that.

They lapsed into silence. A definite chill was falling but they sat on, reluctant to let go of such a rare evening. Finally, Margy stirred to light up another cigarette. "Gene asked me to marry him tonight," she said offhandedly, blowing smoke across the porch. Ralph could feel her eyes on him, trying to read his face in the semidarkness.

"What do you think about that, Ralph?"

"Oh," was all he could say. But yes, he was sure she would do just that, go and live in a place not coloured pink on the calendar map hanging in the kitchen, a place where he was sure he himself would never feel at home. Perhaps he might never even see her again if that happened. There were lots of local girls who had married off to the States, gone as if they had stepped off the face of the earth.

"I know you don't approve of Gene, but he likes you all the same, Ralph. Did you know that? Respects your old-fashioned loyalties, he says."

Quaint was probably what he had said, quaint loyalties. Something like that. Ralph the Quaint, Unsound Mind in Unsound Body.

"Well, we'll look after Edie first. Okay?" She stubbed out her cigarette and got up, hugging herself in the fresh chill, shivering. "Brrr. It's getting 'airsome', as Dad would say. Don't stay out too late, Ralph." She patted his shoulder and went into the house. One of pity, that touch. A sister's fond touch, but full of pity all the same. Loyalties. She wouldn't know he had heard them that night, "An old bitch gone in the teeth," and all that, and her laughing, "Oh, you're terrible, Gene. For God's sake don't let him hear you." And Edie and Olive Penney watching him listen.

Airsome. That was another thing, he thought, with a flash of irritation. What would the folks say, seldom enough visited in the little house on the West Side? Leaving him, she would be, to see to their last days, the dying and all the rest of it. Oh, she might come back for that, a brief appearance, coming back to get what was hers and then be gone again, back to an alien country.

Well, you were whatever you were, and that was that. Sound, unsound, mind, body, one mix or another. 'Unknown Mind, Bad Chest', his own motto. Or 'Bad Luck, Bad Chest'. It was luck, simple and straight, making the world go up or down for you. In the Navy, like Lloyd, except for the chest. A singer, perhaps, of war songs, like the Lieutenant. Or the Artillery, The Royal Newfoundland, like George Caines with the leg all shot up.

Not too much night air, Margy was always warning him. He should go inside, have his sandwich and read a bit waiting up for her. She might even actually walk down with Lloyd but probably not, not the way those two could chat away the hours. He sat on for a while, hands in lap, fingers interlocked, legs stretched out with ankles crossed, tapping out a march beat with the tips of his brogues.

# COLD COMFORT

*I* have certainly had better days than Thursday last. Truth to tell, I'm not sure if I'll ever get over it. Inside that is: heart, soul, psyche, whatever it is.

It happened that my brother-in-law, Paul Matthews, was in Ottawa, as he is three or four times a year, and we had lunch at the Chateau Laurier before he took his afternoon flight back to Toronto. As background, I should tell you that we're members of the Newfoundland diaspora, exiled here in Ontario, myself via a life in the public service, Paul through his consulting work in the chemistry line. He was a city man. I was bred and buttered in Corner Brook. We had become good buddies during the war. When I married my Rose, Paul was the best man, and I was his when — small world — he married Rose's lovely younger sister, Jeanne. Time passed and we were now both widowed. I was childless and retired; he had two lovely daughters.

We decided the weather called for a 'cooler', so there we were, just after noon on a warm August day, two well-grayed specimens with chilled lagers in mind, making our way across the lobby of the Chateau towards the lounge. I caught a second's reflection in a tall mirror by the front desk, averting my eyes from my own central paunch while sourly taking in Paul's still trim and military cut. We had just entered the room, myself in the lead, when Paul roughly grabbed my shoulder, bringing us to a standstill. I heard a sharp intake of breath from him, and when I turned I saw that he was staring openmouthed at this rather attractive lady, a woman with steel-blue hair, in her fifties I would have guessed, sitting alone at the bar, cigarette in hand. Paul swung us both about abruptly, his grasp of my shoulder even firmer.

"Let's skip the drink, George," he whispered urgently.

I was puzzled, as you might imagine, by this odd turn of events. I glanced back as we retreated and saw the mystery woman down the last of her drink, frowning after us over the rim of the glass.

"You look as if you've just seen a ghost, Paul." We had been seated a few minutes in the dining room and had ordered our drinks brought to the table. Paul finished his off with a single gulp, and asked for another. He obviously needed some time to regain his composure and get his thought processes in order, so I ordered for us both, trout for me, roast beef for him, while he sat and stared off into the middle distance. Or into the far distance, as it turned out. Finally, he shook his head, let out a tremulous sigh, and looked at me over interlocked fingers, knuckles as white as the tablecloth.

"Will you hear my confession then, George?"

That sounds ominous, I told him, and I regret it now, playing the priest you might say, especially since I was the last person in the world from whom he could expect forgiveness for this sin.

But, naturally, I was curious. Wouldn't you be? Anyway, here it is, Paul's Story, take it or leave it.

* * *


1955 or '56. You had packed off to Ottawa by then and I was into my Second year teaching chemistry at St. Dunstan's in P.E.I. I was pretty bored, truth to tell, and wondering why in hell I had even accepted the position in the first place. Never meant to be a teacher, that's the truth. Or to live on an island either it seems, the Rock, England, or Prince Edward's. You'd think I'd had enough during the war, but I still hankered for challenges, change, excitement. You'll remember the feeling, George, I'm sure.

Anyway, as luck would have it, in the spring of, oh, say it was '56, I was asked to join a commission looking into the start-up of a full scale university on the Island. I was on a sort of technical subcommittee, and that's how I came to meet Harry Stoneham, who taught English at Prince of Wales College in Charlottetown. Harry was from The Old Country, Yorkshire I think, with a broad twangy accent to match, and I remember teasing him about teaching a language he hadn't learned to speak properly himself. We hit it off and soon took to having a drink or two together after meetings. Eventually he invited me around for dinner one evening. Do you know Charlottetown, George? Well, Harry and his wife had a large old house in the Brighton avenue area, overlooking the harbour.

A Sunday evening in April, one of the coldest springs on record. I walked from my cubbyhole on Euston Street, dark rain clouds over the west of the city, a hard breeze out of the north-west, rigging lights winking and bobbing on a few freighters out in the bay. Oh yes, I remember it all. Still have dreams, in fact, or nightmares might be the better word, about that fateful night.

Harry welcomed me at the door, took my raglan and scarf, then ushered me into the living room. Two other guests had already arrived, Sylvia Doyle, a friend and former student of Harry's, and his next-door neighbour, Farley Cameron. Farley was a well-known local historian and I had met him a couple of times at various events. Greetings and so on were exchanged, cocktails served, and then we sat around chatting, terrible weather and all that. Sylvia, I remember clearly, affording me a very nice view of her well turned legs. She, by the way, chain-smoked these acrid little cigarillos, and when she spoke to me it was in the huskiest voice I have ever heard in a woman.

"Harry tells me you're a chemist, Paul."

I teach it, I told her. "But I do very little real stuff now. Almost none, as a matter of fact."

She supposed, out of a pungent fogbank, that there wasn't a whole lot of research and the like being done on the Island, and I had to agree that was the case, not even in agriculture. Some minor things perhaps, student projects. And you know, George, for some reason, her questions, asked just to make polite conversation mind you, nevertheless cut me to the quick. I was keenly reminded once again of just how peripheral my professional life really was, the whole of my life, in fact. I think she might have sensed that in me, too, judging from the look in her eyes, a shrewd sizing-up, perhaps a touch of pity. A very clever woman, Sylvia Doyle. Very uncomfortable.

Farley was launching into his latest bit of island history, when Harry's wife made her entrance. She excused herself for not being on hand to greet everybody and then was guided towards me, Harry holding her right elbow and saying: "Fran, this is Paul Matthews, the notorious newfie I've told you so much about. Paul — my dear wife, Fran. A fellow Newfoundlander, Paul, Fran is." Now this is where things get really weird, George, but please, hear me out.

Fran put out her hand and I took it, absolutely dumbstruck. I had expected a middle-aged matron, but Fran Stoneham was closer to my own age, even, as I later discovered, two years my junior. You'll scoff, of course, when I say it, but I actually lived the old cliché that evening, George. I fell head over heels in love with Harry Stoneham's 'dear wife' at first sight. And I was sure the feeling was mutual. My hand, after hers had been withdrawn, was actually tingling as if I'd touched a live wire. And I recall — a detail, but I still remember it vividly — that as she withdrew her hand, she curled the fingers into a little fist, and pressed it to her breast as if she too had been stung. Our eyes simply refused to give each other up, and even as she hugged Sylvia I continued to hold her gaze and she mine.

I see you're smiling, George, and I can't say I blame you. I said love, and I agree, the word does get tossed about haphazardly. An infantile fascination, enthrallment, sexual attraction — yes, all those too, I'm sure. And you may wonder, too, if the poor thing simply wasn't thrown for a loop by such gauche behavior on my part. But think what you will, it was there, for us both I was certain, something, some shared connection.

We sat down for dinner, followed by coffee and liqueurs. All through the meal my eyes were drawn to my hostess as if by a magnetic force. I might have made an absolute ass of myself, but I'm fairly sure the others saw nothing untoward in my fascination. Only she acknowledged it, with warm pink blushes along her high cheekbones when our eyes met.

I should say, by the way, that she was not what you would call beautiful. Yes, yes, I know, in the eye of the beholder and all that, but to tell the truth her facial features were a bit irregular actually. The nose, for example, a trifle off centre, I thought. And the left eye, charming in itself, was nevertheless not quite in plumb with the other. But both were dark and lovely, even if they weren't on the level. The mouth too, full lips, a bit pouted, or petulant if you like, sign of a sensuous nature I was sure, or hoped. A nice, assertive jaw line and ears showing like small seashells beneath straight black hair.

We sat and chatted through a haze of cigarette smoke, Sylvia suffocating us with her petite smoke bombs. The talk got around to literature and such, not really my cup of tea. Sylvia was a poet, "learning the trade," as she put it, and Farley, of course, had volume after volume to his credit. "You know, Paul," Harry said, leaning close to my left ear, "Fran writes poetry, too. She's had a bit published, actually." And "Oh yes!" cried Sylvia, overhearing, as Harry no doubt intended, and insisting on a reading. "Your latest, Fran, please?" Farley joined in the urging, and I, meeting her eyes again, said "Yes, please do."

She left the room for a minute and returned with a small book in hand, a diary or the like, black leather, sealed with a small silver clasp. "Just the one," she insisted. "You weren't asked here to listen to my poor verses. This one will be in the next *Fiddlehead* by the way, so it's a bit of a scoop for you, if you like." She opened her little book slowly, almost reverently you might say, like a priest uncovering a chalice.

I used to know that poem by heart, George. Had a copy of that *Fiddlehead* too, signed by her of course. A fond inscription, too, "To my naughty fellow newfie," or the like. All gone now, lost in the mists of time, as they say. I remember, though, that it dealt with love, about how, between lovers, betrayal is almost inevitable, an inherent element of the human condition, you might say. I was sure she had decided to read it for my benefit, although I couldn't be sure what the message it held for me. That she would not betray? That she would?

The enchanted evening ended and I walked Sylvia Doyle back downtown, taking advantage of the opportunity to find out more about my new found land of love, Fran Stoneham. She hailed from around your neck of the woods, George, in the Townsite area I think she called it, and had graduated with honours from Mount Allison. Harry had been one of her professors. "He's twenty or twenty five years older, you know," Sylvia informed me. Oh yes, and she considered Fran's poetry to be "interesting", or perhaps "promising" was the word she used.

I saw quite a bit of the Stonehams after that. For reasons I still can't understand, I seemed to fit in with their 'crowd': academic types mostly, the city's artistic and bookish fringe, such as it was, a sprinkling of senior public servants and the like included for good measure. It was at Farley Cameron's place at Cavendish where Fran and I had our first physical encounter. First and last, actually. Farley had put on some old Fats Waller stuff on the gramophone, *Two Sleepy People, I Can't Give You Anything But Love*, slow, easy dance music. I was relaxing with a cool drink when Harry leaned over the back of the lounge chair and touched my shoulder. "Would you be good enough to dance with Fran, Paul? Touch of the gout tonight, I'm afraid."

His face was grey and strained and he really did seem to be in some discomfort. I eagerly agreed, naturally, and looked at Fran and she didn't hesitate to come into my arms as if ... oh, how can I put it, George ... well, as if it had been ordained, shall we say, as if we had been separated in a distant past by some cosmic blunder that was finally to be put right. Her hand in mine was soft yet strong. I could feel the smoothness of her slender body moving under the silk of her summer blouse, and her fingers along my shoulder exerted a delicious, intimate pressure. I reacted, of course, couldn't help it, and she knew it too. Her eyes half closed and she sighed and moved her pelvis from side to side ever so slightly, pushing gently against me. Thank God she had had the good sense to steer us into the semi-darkness of the screened porch or else I'm sure we would have caused a scandal.

"Fran ..." I began earnestly, but she pulled away from me, whispering "Hush, Paul, hush." I tried to regain possession but she put the palm of her hand against my mouth and shook her head, her lips rounding a silent firm No! Not an absolute no, of that I was certain, just a reminder that time and place were awry, and then she went to look after Harry, leaving me to smoke a cigarette and cool off in the gulf breeze.

We were thrown together like that from time to time. So close, so often, and yet she never yielded, only gave the impression that she might, just might, surrender if and when. In dozens of small ways, deliberate and otherwise, she kept me captivated. When playing Bridge, for example, she had a way, when making a point, of reaching across the card table and covering the back of one's hand with hers, and when she touched mine I was sure it was given to me alone.

I remember running into her one afternoon in the library on Grafton Street, where I was brushing up on my poetry, adding another siege weapon to my armory.

We had coffee together and she told me something about her upbringing in Newfoundland. Her folks were actually from Minnesota, moving to Corner Brook when the Americans built the mill there. "They're back in the States now," she told me. "Dad retired a while back. But after twenty-five years that seems to have been a mistake. They really miss Newfoundland. So do I."

I asked her how she came by her interest in writing poetry and it seems she had gotten a love of the stuff from her mother, whose verses had often appeared in the *Western Star.* There had also been a soft-cover collection printed once, which had been well received, even in St. John's.

Then there was this awkward silence. I was on the verge of openly pleading my passion when she touched the back of my hand and shook her head slowly and firmly, as if she had sensed my intention. "I love Harry," she said. A simple statement, all that needed to be said I suppose. Yet there it was, George, in her eyes, in the press of her fingers on my wrist, the silent plea for my continuing the game. We held hands for a minute, I said nothing more, and she picked up her books and handbag and left, looking as miserable, I thought, as I felt.

Things had to be resolved, of course. Insanely in love, hopelessly infatuated, whatever it was, I was on the verge of doing something horribly rash and juvenile to bring things to a head. So many complications, George, as you can imagine. First of all, Harry was a friend, a good one, and I couldn't simply jump into bed with his wife as if there was nothing else to it. I knew too, that a relationship with Fran Stoneham would carry with it a total commitment, a total change of life, with divorce, marriage, family and mutual friend problems, the whole ball of wax, you might say. But there I was, caught up in the grand passion of my life. She was my Beatrice, my Isolde, my Juliette. What to do? What could I do, George? What would you have done?

But events overtake us, as they say, and thank God they do. A day or so after the library thing, Harry told me the committee was sending a group on a tour of several other provinces, as well as to one or two states. New degree factories had opened in British Columbia and Ontario, as well as in California and Florida, and the Minister had decided we might learn a useful thing or two on such a jaunt. Harry was supposed to go, but had begged off because of his health problems. He had not easily, as he told me quite frankly, persuaded the reluctant powers-that-be to let me stand in for him. The Minister, he joked, distrusted anyone under forty, and seemed to think education was largely wasted on the young anyway. "Perhaps he's right," he added with a grin. Then he put his hand on my arm. "Look, could I have a word with you later on, Paul? Can you come around to the house tonight, say about eight or so?"

When I got to Harry's place that evening I found him looking very much under the weather. Really sick looking, truth to tell, and I realized that, obsessed with Fran, I had been pushing Harry further and further into the background, wishing him not to be there at all, I suppose. He went to freshen up, telling me to make a drink for myself, nothing for him, so I poured an inch of scotch and added water in the kitchen.

"I look like hell, don't I?" Harry said when he came back. He looked a bit off, I told him. Too much committee work, perhaps?

"I'm dying, Paul," he said, matter-of-factly. "That's

the truth of it, I'm afraid." Turns out he'd had a malignant tumor cut out of his lower abdomen about three years prior. Damn thing was back, despite the radiation and chemotherapy and all the rest of it. "Couldn't cope with the university any longer. Everybody was kind, of course, got me fixed up here with a lighter workload and all. Minister is an old *Mount A.* man, you know."

He wanted a favour of me, a fairly simple one. He and Fran would be moving to Halifax in a month or so and they were wondering if I would be good enough to move into the house while they were away. Rent free, of course. With Farley away so much, it would be a relief for them to have a reliable friend on the premises and so on. Fran, he said, had especially wanted him to ask me. I agreed numbly.

Well, you can imagine how I felt, George. Absolutely disgusted with myself, totally dismayed by the way I'd been carrying on. While I had been trying to seduce his wife, Harry, a good friend if ever there was one, had been struggling painfully, heroically if you like, against this implacable enemy. To be betrayed by his body was at least natural and understandable, however unfortunate, but to be betrayed by a friend? That was unnatural, George. Bad form, as Harry himself would to say.

I avoided close contact with Fran after that. Saw her once or twice at this or that gathering, and our eyes would meet as usual. I thought her expression accusing and hurt, but something held me back from going to her, and I would take my leave as soon as possible, full of distaste for the feelings I still had for her. And then the trip was on, thank God, and the traveling circus was off, British Columbia our first stop.

The travel was numbing, yet at the same time consoling. My head was still full of her, but distance seemed to make the heart grow less agitated. We talked with MPPs and MPs, congressmen and senators, administrators, rectors, chancellors and presidents, rafts of bureaucrats, and on the flight between San Francisco and Miami I decided I had to leave Prince Edward Island. Our last stop was in Sudbury. I went to Toronto from there and had a number of interviews with potential employers. Almost six weeks had gone by when I got back to Charlottetown with a job offer in my pocket.

There were loose ends to tie up during the next week or so: resigning from my teaching post, tidying up my papers and paying bills and so on, getting my old Chev serviced, arranging a caretaker for the Stoneham's house. Minutiae. It was a relief to know that Harry was being treated in Halifax and that I wouldn't be bumping into Fran on some street corner. The only incident that sticks out in my mind was something that happened, or something I imagined happened, when I went to see Fred Kendall — the Minister of Education at the time — at his potato farm out in Kensington. I owed it to him to convey my resignation from the committee in person and I wanted to hand him a short 'ex officio' report I'd put together on the junket findings.

Fred was polite and he didn't seem too devastated by the loss of my services. We had a cup of tea and when I was taking my leave he brought up Harry Stoneham's situation. He had a high regard for Harry but he didn't think there was much could be done for him now. And then he added: "I feel sorry for her too, for the wife. Perhaps there's something *I* could do for her." Perhaps I imagined it, but I was sure he stressed the personal pronoun and that the look he gave me was,

well, accusing, disapproving. As a matter of fact, I felt
I was getting a lot of looks like that from a lot of the
acquaintances and friends I'd shared with the Stonehams.
It was a small town, Charlottetown, and I guess I'd
been a bit of a fool to think my feelings had gone
unnoticed. Or hers, it would seem.

All the way to Toronto I turned it over and over
in my mind. I didn't feel I had any particular obligation
to Harry, who was no doubt surrounded by closer
friends than myself, but had I failed Fran? Had I
abandoned her in an hour of need? … allowed some
unworthy puritan impulse, some niggling hairsplitting
doubts to persuade me into betrayal? I was pursued
by a demon of remorse, and for months her face, her
accusing look, haunted my dreams.

I was in Toronto for three or four months when I
learned Harry had died. Farley Cameron sent a copy
of the obit from *The Guardian*. Fran was the sole family
member left to mourn. Her maiden name? Funny sort
of name, I remember. Halfpenny, I think. Or Halpenny.
Ring a bell, George? Anyway, no other kin, apparently,
here or in England. I felt that pang again, but now I
could throw myself into my new work and that helped.
It was four or five years later before I heard anything
more about Fran, and by then I was married to Jeanne
and twice a father.

I ran into Sylvia Doyle one lunchtime in the Eaton
Centre. We kissed and hugged and went somewhere
to have a coffee. She was Sylvia Cooper at this time,
you may have heard of her, and in town for a reading
or the like. We chatted about Charlottetown, where she
still lived, mutual friends and so on. "Do you remember
Fran Stoneham, Paul?" she asked, lighting up one of
those noxious cigarillos, and I felt such a sudden pain

in my chest, George, at the mere mention of her name. "Fran," I replied weakly. "Yes. Yes, of course."

Fran had remarried, a terrible business as it turned out. "I don't think she knew what to do, after poor Harry died. Ended up with a lout named Clive Marsh, from around Antigonish, I believe. Failed artist type. Punched her around now and then, drank like a fish, and then did the only decent bit of work he'd ever done. Ran his car off the road one night and broke his neck. Good riddance, too."

"Any children?"

She looked at me in that calculating manner of hers. "No. But tell me, Paul. Didn't you two … ? Well, we always thought you and she, you know, had a sort of thing going, shall we say."

"Where is she now?" I asked, my face, I'm sure, an open book to the prescient Sylvia. "How is she? Does she still write poetry?"

She had kept in touch with Fran actually, in an off-and-on sort of way. Fran had not married again and eventually had gone to live with her aging parents in Minnesota. In St. Paul, and wasn't that an interesting coincidence? St. Paul, Paul? And yes, she still wrote and had a piece published now-and-then.

How I wished I had never run into Sylvia Cooper. It all came back, George, with a vengeance, my passion for Fran, like the return of Harry's cancer. Not that I was unhappily married, as you well know, but after that lunchtime reawakening, the old obsession once again invaded my day-to-day existence. Jeanne's place in my life was usurped by this phantom, this imagined presence as real to me as if it had been there in the flesh. A ghost figure, but one that created an overwhelming longing in me and gave me a despairing sense of having incurred a profound loss. I called out her name once, dreaming, and I remember Jeanne laughing at me for crying out "France!" in my sleep. And even when I looked at the girls, George, God forgive me, I used to wonder what they would have looked like, what sort of characters they would have had, had their mother been Fran. When Jeanne died, everybody said I was taking it well. I think you said as much yourself, George. Well, now you know why, I suppose.

Anyway, there you are, my friend. My true confession. Good for the soul, I suppose, as you Catholics say. You asked if I had seen a ghost? Yes, George, and one I have lived with for thirty years. To see her like that. So suddenly, so … changed.

* * *

That was Paul's story. I sat looking at him as if at a total stranger.

"Such a long time," I said numbly. "Can you really be sure?"

"I'm sure it's her, George. Absolutely. I should tell you that Sylvia has sent me a few bits and pieces over the years. A photo of her with Fran at some university reading, the two of them on a boat somewhere. That sort of thing. Oh yes, I'm sure it's her."

It's a long story, but Jeanne Matthews had been a soul mate to me, like a sister I could share a few secrets with, closer to me in some ways than Rose could ever have been. I remembered how hard her cruel early death had been for me to accept and I did not much like the newly-shrived sinner sitting across from me.

"Perhaps it's not too late," I suggested. After all, I

pressed on, she is probably still in the lounge, so why not put the ghost to rest? And who knows, she may still hold that grand passion in her own heart. "Love at our age is as sweet as it is at two and twenty, George. So they say."

"She would not have forgiven me," he murmured, shaking his head. There was an inch or two of the house red left in the bottle. I topped up our glasses. "You would be no worse off, George. Go ahead. I'll look after things here." But he continued to fidget, tiny beads of sweat popping out along his receding hairline.

"You may put two ghosts to rest, Paul."

He frowned. "Two ghosts, George?"

"Don't forget Jeanne's," I said, with a bitterness that seemed to go right over his head. But he downed the last of his wine, rose resolutely, threw his napkin on the table with a dramatic flourish, and I watched him stride purposefully out of the dining room, memories of Jeanne Matthews flooding my mind. Paul's life with her had been an ongoing act of betrayal, a sustained lie worse than barefaced adultery, a sort of spiritual desertion. How true Dante had been about Hell, I thought, putting betrayers in the lowest depths. Absolution denied, Paul.

He was back in a minute or so. She wasn't there and the bartender thought she had been part of tour group that had left a half-hour ago. Which bus? Who could say, there were so many. He was actually shaking with relief and I felt a surge of disappointment that he had escaped possible retribution.

"You should check at the desk," I suggested. "She might be registered here."

"Yes. Oh, I did, George, I did. She is not."

But I was sure he had not. Perhaps he had not

even gone into the lounge. He had a three o'clock flight back to Toronto so I left him at the elevators and made my way back to my apartment on Bay Street. I fed the Siamese its breakfast, something I had forgotten to do that morning. I don't like cats much but I had kept Simon because Rose had doted on him.

Then I looked up the number in the directory and rang it from the bedroom, watching myself in the dresser mirror, a short, overweight, aging person seated on an empty bed.

"Reservations. May I help you?" Then the same *en français*.

"Look, I wonder if you have a Mrs. Frances Marsh registered there?"

I waited a few seconds. "No sir. No one by that name."

"Wait, wait. Perhaps a Frances Hapenny? Or Halfpenny? From Minnesota?"

Another pause. Yes sir, they did indeed have an F. Halfpenny registered. Did I wish to ring her room?

No, I said, thank you. I replaced the receiver, frowning at my reflection. The Siamese poked its head around the bedroom door and meowed. "Well now," I asked it, "and what would you make of that, I wonder."

I rang the hotel again, getting a different voice at the desk. "You have a Miss Frances Halfpenny registered there. Would you give her room a ring for me, please?"

There were three rings and I thought, well, she is probably on a tour bus and off to see some museum or visit Parliament Hill. But on the fourth the receiver was lifted and a woman said, a bit tremulously I thought, "Hello?"

"Is this Frances Halfpenny? From Corner Brook, Newfoundland?"

Hesitation, naturally. "Yes?"

"You don't know me, Miss Halfpenny, but my name is George Caines, and I used to live in Corner Brook, too. On the West Side, actually and …"

She interrupted to ask how I knew who she was and how I knew she was in Ottawa. I could feel her puzzlement through the receiver. Who was this, she must have been wondering, this unknown voice in an unknown city. I thought I caught a slur in her voice too, as if she might be just a bit tipsy.

"I think we have a mutual friend, Miss HalfPenney. Paul Matthews?"

"Who?"

"I think you knew him in Charlottetown. I guess you were Frances Stoneham at the time. Quite a while ago?"

"What is this? Who are you?" There was an edge of, not fear exactly, but of uneasiness in her voice now.

"Paul Matthews. He was a teacher at St. Dunstan's College at the time and he worked with your husband, Professor Stoneham … on some government committee? Paul Matthews?"

Her tone took on a distinctly suspicious flavouring and grew firmer. "I have not lived in Charlottetown for thirty years, Mr … I'm afraid I didn't catch … Caines, yes … and then I think I was there for about two years at the most. I'm sorry, but I don't recall anyone of that name. Matthews, did you say?"

Then there was a pause and I distinctly heard a sharp intake of breath, and could imagine the look of alarm that must have spread over her face. "Is he that fellow … in the lounge today? The one that gave me such a start?" The nervousness was now unmistakable.

"Matthews," I repeated lamely. "Look, I am very sorry for bothering you, Miss Halfpenny. It seems a mistake has been made and believe me there is no cause for alarm. Just a case of mistaken identity it seems."

I cradled the phone and contemplated the unpleasantly exultant image in the mirror. Simon the Siamese (it scans, Rose used to say) had vaulted to the bed and had staked out an unchallenged claim on the counterpane. It lay felinely with paws folded under narrow breast, blue tail coiled about a lean bluish flank. I raised my eyebrows in mute inquiry but the beast only yawned, shrugged, and half-closed its cold indifferent eyes.

*Tom Finn*

# QUIGLEY'S LUCK

## BOOZEY'S PROLOGUE

*I*s it 'luck' I hear you going on about over there? Well here. Have a couple on the house then, gentlemen, and let me tell you about Kevin Quigley's dearly departed old dad, Pius Quigley, God rest his soul, and the strange thing that happened to him just after the war was over. This comes right from the horse's mouth, too, right from Monsignor Kevin himself, told to me before he was even ordained, let alone raised to the exalted corner he now finds himself in. We called him Quick Quigley back then, Kevin I mean, or usually just 'The Quick' or 'Quicky', because he had the sharp tongue on him and the sharp head to go along with it too. No doubt he still has, I'm sure, although to tell the truth I haven't had two words with the good man these ten years or more now.

The thirties it was, the 'Dirty Thirties' as they're called, when the Quigleys were living way up on Stratton's Road, two streets over from our house on the West Side of Corner Brook. Hard times they were too, I can tell you. My own Dad, who had the loveliest pen you could ever find, hung on to his job at the paper mill, while The Quick, who was more of a common sort of outdoor labourer, wasn't so fortunate and soon found himself on the dole. Things were pretty grim for the Quigleys for a spell, until one fine day, thanks be to God, Pius got taken on as a deckhand with the Furness-Withy people in St. John's. I expect you may have heard of Captain Frank Reddy, another good man lost in the Merchant Marine? Well,

Pius' brother-in-law Frank Reddy was First Mate on the *SS Dromore* at the time, where he was able, as he did, to put in a good word for Pius when it counted.

Now the West Side, as you will know if you know anything about Corner Brook, was what you might call the poor side of the town, as compared to the Townsite, across the brook on the east side, which had been planned and built, and was owned and run by the paper mill company. And on the West Side there were parts that weren't too bad, all in all, and other parts that were. Being that we were close to the main drag, where water and sewer lines had lately been put in, our house had inside plumbing, while a lot of others, the Quigleys for one, had no services at all save for the hydro. Folks had to get their water from dug wells that got polluted every time it rained, which was often enough, ensuring regular outbreaks of measles and mumps and typhoid fever and scarlet fever, not to mention diphtheria and dysentery and just about every other catching disease and ailment known to man. Not a time of year, except perhaps in the cold heart of winter, but somebody on our street didn't have their house posted with the yellow quarantine notice, with nobody allowed in or out of the place for whatever time it took to get rid of the plague inside. And then afterwards you couldn't walk past the house without your nose stinging from the sulphur stink of the fumigating. Open ditches ran down the sides of most roadways on the West Side, and I can tell you, you wouldn't want to be taking your Saturday night bath in one of them either.

But the worst part of the West Side, no argument about it, was what we called Crow Gulch, a clutch of tarpaper shacks down by the pulpwood booms that looked as if they might have been tossed up on shore by a tidal wave or the like. There was no road down to Crow Gulch, only a hard stony footpath; no services, not even the hydro, and all hard rock it was, too, so you couldn't even think to dig a well. Whatever fresh water they got came down from a spring up in the cliffs above the Curling road, carried down by a rubber hose that often as not was blocked up or frozen or pulled out altogether by some mischief maker. We were cruel as children, and I remember we used to pee into that spring pool and laugh about what the jackytars down the hill would be drinking in their tea for supper. A jackytar, if any of you aren't familiar with the term, was the lowest caste of person in Newfoundland at the time, which is saying something, let me tell you; a mix, as I understand it, of Micmac and French blood from the times when the French more or less owned, or at least had the use of, the west coast of the Island. We used to be kept in line with threats of having the jackytars being put after us, or being sent down to live in Crow Gulch and no matter how badly off you might be, there was always the consolation of thinking: *At least I'm not a jackytar, thank God, and have to live in Crow Gulch!*

The point? Well, the point, you see, is that Pius Quigley's bit of luck, and The Quick's too as it turned out, had all to do with a family named Bougoise, *boo-gees* we used to pronounce it, and that's where they came out of, out of Crow Gulch.

Now in this family, the Boogees, the mother would have been long dead by the time Quigley's story starts, from the TB or the typhoid or a mix of both. I think there was a young girl too, I don't recall her name, but she died early on, thirteen or so, of the

TB too, most likely. The father was called Youvey, Youvey Boogee; and there was a little fellow, Jerry, who used to turn up now and then at Our Mother of Perpetual Help School over on Caribou Road. I remember we were always warned not to sit next to Jerry Boogee, if we could help it, for fear of catching the nits off him.

Anyway ... here, let me top that up for you ... anyway, with Pius away so much, this Youvey Boogee, in one way or another, got to helping out Mary Quigley with the chores, because she was having a bit of a rough time with the four kids they already had, not to mention the one on the way, and not a man about the place when she needed a hand. It started out when he came across her chopping up the splits one frosty morning, and doing it as clumsy as could be, being as she was seven months along with number five. So he offered to do it for her and she gladly agreed and, then, when he was all done, she gave him a ten cent piece for his trouble. After that he began to turn up almost on a regular basis, Pius home or Pius away, and they always found something for him to do, even if it was something that didn't need doing at all, the Quigleys being nothing if not Christian to a fault.

Now one fine spring day, the young fellow, Jerry, came tagging along with his dad, and Mrs. Quigley was so filled up with pity for the little fellow, skinny as a pitchfork and with the big dark eyes and the curly black hair on him, that she pulled him straight into the house and made him put down a decent home cooked scoff for what might have been the first time in his short miserable life. This turned into a regular thing too, and to be honest I don't think young Jerry Boogee would have lived to see his teens except for the Quigleys feeding him up like that two or three times a week. I really don't, because poor Youvey himself was soon into the San with the consumption and when he came out of that place, I'm sorry to say, he wasn't the least bit alive. The end result was that little Jerry was double-orphaned at eleven or twelve years of age without a single soul in the whole wide world that could or would lay claim to him. The Quick claimed he begged his folks to take the orphan in, and I'm sure that's the truth, but with five of their own to feed and clothe it would have overstretched even the Quigleys' good hearts to undertake such a thing, an extra soul to care for in those hard times. What finally happened, thanks to the Redemptorists, the good Father O'Hara especially, was the lad ended up with the Christian Brothers at the famous — or the infamous as it is now I suppose — Mount Cashel Orphanage in St. John's.

I'll have to shift gears a bit at this point because a few years have to go by and, there's a change of scene, as well, from Corner Brook to dear old St. John's. I'm trying too, as I hope you can tell, not to turn things into a sermon or the like, which was a thing The Quick was inclined to do when he got to telling stories, always tending to turn them into parables or morality plays or whatever, a habit I always found irritating. Drive you up the wall the way he could go on trying to twist things into theological knots. But Lord, the man could talk all the same, let me tell you. Yes, a lovely talker and mimic, The Quick, and he first spun this one, to me at least, when he was home from his first year at St. FX and the two of us had come out to do a bit of fishing at Flat Bay Brook, a lovely little salmon river that runs out of the

Long Range Mountains, making pool after lovely pool before it runs into the salty waters of Bay St. George. We were boiling up the small grilse I'd landed late in the afternoon, the only thing we hooked on the trip, by the way, and which was the reason we got to talking about luck in the first place. And what follows is what Monsignor 'The Quick' Quigley told to me that soft summer evening, sitting alongside that sweet little stream, the waters purling away nearby, the breeze sighing in the trees about, a wood fire crackling under the pot. Ah, as me-own mother would say, rest her soul, *God be with the days*, eh?

## THE PRIEST'S TALE

Now where was it you left off? Oh, yes, in St. John's, three or four years later on.

The bleak year of 1936, it was. or perhaps it was '37, not that it makes much difference. A bitter November night, a Saturday night, the wind whistling in through the Narrows and banking up off the harbour waters, gusting up the hilly roadways, carrying along with it that raw salty cold off the North Atlantic that gets into your very bones and sets your eyes watering and your teeth chattering. Dad and Uncle Frank Reddy were making their way back to the *Dromore*, beating downhill from the Basilica where they had just gone to confession, and were almost in sight of the vessel which was tied up, naturally, at the Furness-Withy pier. They had only the length of the Ayer's Cove laneway left to navigate before emerging onto the wharf when it happened. Out of the dark of an alleyway corner came a wail, a pitiful cry that startled the living daylights, or nightlights in this case I suppose, right out of the two newly-shriven penitents. "Mr. Quigley!" someone in obvious distress called out to them, "Mr. Quigley! Give us a hand here, Mr. Quigley, for the love of God, give us a hand!"

You'll have guessed who it was, I'm sure. None other than little Jerry Boogee himself, only not nearly as small, of course, nor nearly as cherubic either, with more than a few more pounds over the bones and a foot or more in height to help carry them. All the same, Dad had no trouble at all telling straight-off who it was. "Jerry! Goodness gracious, my son, what's the matter with you at all?"

The poor fellow looked like death warmed over, shaking like a leaf, wearing only a thin summer jacket, and with a small school cap of some sort stuck over the black curly hair. His face was pinched with the cold, his shoulders trembling in the bitter night wind. He was clearly close to total collapse so it was decided then and there to take him on board to thaw him out and as they were helping him climb up the gangplank, didn't the wind come up in a sudden gust and take the little cap right off his frozen head, sending it spinning off into the dark harbour waters. "Oh let it go," gasped Jerry, "just let it go, boys. It's not me own, anyway." Mark that well, now Boozy, the wind and the cap. "Not me own," says Jerry Boogee, "not me own!"

Later on, after a rum floater, followed by

boiled tea and a plate of raisin buns from the galley, their unexpected guest had ceased shaking and shivering and was finally ready to throw some light on his obviously desperate situation. And listen, why don't I let Jerry himself take over here, Boozy, to make sure we get a faithful rendering of his side of things? I see you nodding agreement, so I will, passing along to you in his own way and words what was told to Dad and Uncle Frank Reddy on that bitter November night in St. John's harbour.

## INTERJECTION BY BOOZY

This was one of The Quick's little dodges when he was spinning a tale where the subject matter got a little too, well, delicate, let us say, for clerical comfort. Getting a layman to do the dirty work, I called it. A 'rhetorical device' was his terminology. No matter, I suppose.

## THE ORPHAN'S TALE

First of all, let me say this, if you don't mind. I got on real good at Cashel, and that's the God's truth of it, too. Oh yes, a hard lot, the Brothers were, and wouldn't they dish out a clap alongside your head if they thought you needed it, oh indeed they would. But when you came out of the kind of place I did, and with not a soul in the country you could call even a cousin, it was a real step up in the world, believe me. Three meals a day, a warm bed, and a chance to learn something into the bargain. Oh yes, I liked it okay and I got along well enough with the Brothers, too, and hardly had a complaint at all about the place.

So there I was, like the Monsignor was saying, in a cabin on the *SS Dromore*, all warmed up safe-and-sound for the time being, but more than likely with the whole of the St. John's constabulary all about town on the lookout for me. I wish you could have seen their faces when I told them that, because you know how straitlaced Frank Reddy was, and Mr. Quigley, of course, with the wife and kids back in Corner Brook, the last thing he would be needing was trouble with the law and, God forbid, having his livelihood put in danger. Now for God's sake, don't be getting yourselves all worked up, I told them, because it's not for murder they're after me, nor for robbery or the like.

The thing was, I was supposed to have got this girl in trouble, you see, got her knocked up like. And her old man, Mr. Albert Pink, he was out to kill me for sure. This girl had two brothers, too, hard as nails the both of them. Real soccer toughs, through and through Orangemen to boot, always ready to beat up on any mick that gave then half a reason, let alone one that was having it off with their own sister. Well, that's bad enough, says Mr. Quigley and Frank Reddy, but still they wanted to know, how come the cops were mixed up in it all? Why was it any of their business then? Because I swore up and down to them, and it was the Lord's own truth too, that she wasn't underage or anything like that, no, no, nothing like that involved, nor that she wasn't willing or anything either, that was for sure.

Let's do another backup then, so I can put in another thing about Cashel. It was there that I got started in the carpentry business. The Brothers early on took special notice of how clever I was with the tools, with the woodworking and all, a real natural at it they said I was, which I suppose must be something I got from the old man, who was the real handyman, as Mr. Quigley well knew. And it was something I loved doing too, the best thing of all about Mount Cashel for me. So anyway, when I was about sixteen going-on-seventeen, the Brothers got me a part-time job with an old *St. Bon's* boy, Mr. Peter Cleary, a general fixer-upper and jack-of-all-trades who had a shop of sorts out on the Manuel's Road. They figured that with enough experience under my belt I could get my own papers; so there I was, set for three days a week out at Peter's place, Sunday night through to Wednesday.

We got along good, Peter Cleary and myself, and I don't suppose you could find a better soul to work for in the whole of Newfoundland. Taught me a wonderful lot of tricks, all the finer points of the trade and so on, and after a year or so he would often say to me, and he said it to the Brothers too, that there wasn't much left for him to show me anymore. He even said that things had turned all about and that often as not it was now me teaching him a thing or two. Born for it, they all said I was, and who knows, maybe I was, if I was born for anything at all. I was moved in with Peter, whose wife was dead ten years or more, since he had a spare bedroom and was relying more and more on me to do most of the work that came in.

It was about this time that this Mr. Albert Pink that I mentioned before came into the picture. I don't know if you've ever heard of the man, but he was newly come into the city with his whole family, lock, stock and barrel, from Bonavista, I think it was, or somewhere like that. The wife was supposed to have some old Bonavista Bay money behind her, that's what was told to me anyway, and he was going to set himself up as a shipping agent and that sort of thing, freight handling and insurance and the like. He was setting up shop over on New Gower Street and needed the bottom floor done over, with shelves and counters and partitions and so on. He hired Peter Cleary for the job, and it was decided between them that I would go over to do the actual work. Pink and the bunch of them were living upstairs but I could bunk out in the basement snug enough, says he, and if there was anything I couldn't handle on my own Peter could always be called on to help out. Great experience, you see, for a young carpenter, a full week of work, with six dollars in wages and free board to-boot.

Frank Reddy allowed he'd heard of Albert Pink all right, but he had a hard time wondering how the job would have gone to Peter Cleary in the first place. Oh, don't you worry, I told him, don't you worry, Albert Pink might be as Orange as King Billy, but he'd hire on the Pope himself if it meant saving a dollar or two, because the going rate, as you might well know yourself, is more like ten dollars for a week's work like that. So there you are, question answered.

Fresh and early then, on a raw Monday morning, I started in at Pink's new shop. But by Wednesday it was pretty clear the job wouldn't be done in a week. It couldn't be, because there was almost never anything in the way of materials on hand. As it turned out, Pink nor his missus didn't have much Bonavista Bay money behind them after all, old or new, nor money from any other bay come to that, and there wasn't a supplier in town that would have anything but cash on the barrel-head from them either. Two whole weeks went by with the job only half-done and I was getting pretty tired of sitting around twiddling my thumbs and hardly a dime in my pocket to buy a smoke even. When the third week rolled along I went out to Peter Cleary's and complained about not seeing a bit of my wages, and bye and bye Pink's missus came down to the basement and handed me three dollars.

What's this, I says to her, pardon me ma'am, but its supposed to be six dollars the week ain't it? and she says *Yes, so it is, but it's the common practice to hold back the wages until the job is finished and done to the employer's satisfaction. When the job was done,* she says, *then the rest would be paid and not before.* But when I asks her how I could get the job done if there's nothing to do it with, she only shrugs and says that wasn't *any of her business* and goes off up the stairs.

So here I was, into the third week of this one-week job, wandering about, down to the wharf or up to Signal Hill, waiting for Albert Pink to get some more cash in his hands and worrying if I'd ever see a cent of what he owed me. Anyway, you know what they say about idle hands and the devil, and sure enough, it wasn't long before he caught sight of me fiddling about and rigged up some trouble for me to get into.

Like I said, the Pinks had the two sons, Phil and Will, hard as nails, and I used to keep myself totally out of their way. But there was also a girl, Violet was her name, who used to bring me down my supper most nights, fish and potatoes, bread and tea, rice pudding if I was lucky. She was just turned eighteen, so she told me anyway, and plainer than a slab of salt cod, with a nose you could crochet a doily with and this sharp mean little mouth with no lips to it hardly at all. Her face was kind of splotchy, too, and her eyes were a bit too close together it seemed to me, like her head might have got caught in a nut-cracker or something. All the same, and you couldn't deny it, she was otherwise certainly well put together, as I couldn't help noticing.

Now this Violet was usually what you might call distant whenever she was dealing with me, very superior-acting you might say, sort of looking down the length of her nose like I was from the moon or somewhere. I think she was a bit surprised finding out that a Cashel boy had regular arms and legs just like her own crowd did and that I could even talk English to her about as well as she could herself. And then one night it was my turn to be surprised, because she stayed on after putting the tray down, standing in the doorway to my little cubbyhole and watching me eat.

*You're a Roman then, aren't you?*

I guess I am, I allowed.

She takes to leaning up against the doorframe, looking a bit idle and mischievous. She wonders aloud:

*What's it like then, going to the confession? I couldn't ever do that, telling a man about, you know, things.*

Yes, she was the bold one, let me tell you. It was pretty clear what was on her mind, too, and it wasn't theology either, you could bet the family schooner on that. Never came right out with it, of course, not at the start anyway, but I could see what she was really interested in from the smirk on her face and the way she was sizing me up. Right on the edge of her tongue it was.

*Is it the truth, do you know, what they say about them nuns? In the convents there, with the priests and all that? My Dad got this book written by a nun up in Quebec, up in Canada, and he says it's the real truth too, printed up with pictures and everything.*

Boys, but you could see how she getting all worked up, the eyes flashing at me, the face burning.

*I heard Jewish girls can do it with anyone at all as much as they want to and its only a sin if they don't marry another Jew. Is that the truth do you know?*

Well, it was her going on like that, that did it I guess, gave the devil his opening you might say. When she bends over to take up the tray I runs my hand up the back of her legs, all the way up to her behind, and truth to tell I don't know who was the more surprised, her or me. It was a damn reckless thing for me to do, that's for sure. One yell out of her and them two brothers would have come charging down the stairs and likely as not murder me there and then. But I'm only human, after all, and she was well inclined to it, as I'm sure you'll agree, and on top of everything else I was pretty fed up with Albert Pink by this time and I'm sure that had something to do with it too. Anyway, all she did was give out a little gasp and take to shivering and then we had a go at it, kissing and feeling around each other. It turned out she was no stranger to the business, either, and it was clear enough I wasn't the first one to have a go at her, no siree, nor the second or more for that matter. Bold as a two-dollar whore down on the Battery she was, but we had to break off pretty quick because her Mum would soon be back from visiting Mrs. Martin next door and she had go to a Guides meeting that night. *But I'd rather* … she whispered in my ear and then took off upstairs.

And did she ever rather. Let me tell you. I'm sorry, Mr. Reddy, I don't mean to embarrass anybody, but you got to understand how it was. Mr. Quigley, you know what I mean, being a married man and all. She came sneaking back after a half-hour or so in her Guides outfit, which soon came off and there was nothing shrinking about this Violet I can tell you. Her looks didn't matter a bit to me, the pimples or the mouth like kissing a bit of cracked linoleum, because the lighting was dim and low and, like I said, the rest of her was cobbled together pretty nice, boys, pretty nice for sure. It was like getting caught in a blizzard, if you know what I mean, like being in a firestorm sort of thing, and the neither of us took any care of any sort, no precautions taken at all, never even gave it the slightest thought.

There were two or three more times after that, and she was always as mad for it as she was the first time. I got a bit frightened by her, truth to tell, not so much as being found out, though that was always in the back of my mind, but by the way she was, she was always so hungry to be going at it all the time. It was like it was the only thing in her life, doing it and doing it, like some kind of sickness, maybe, or something. At the same time, I won't pretend I was trying to avoid her or anything, because she sure knew how to get me going too. It's just that, well, when the job got finished, four weeks behind time, I wasn't unhappy in the least to get the hell out of the place, and that's no lie.

Well, I was back with Peter Cleary for a couple of months or so when there was a call for me to go over and see Albert Pink. I suppose warning bells should have gone off in my head, but all I thought about was the wages he still owed me, about forty dollars in all, and naturally that was what I figured he wanted to see me for. The fling with Violet was long behind and totally finished as far as I was concerned and I was sure it was the same thing for her and that you could bet your bottom dollar she'd be at it with someone else by this time.

So I made my way over to New Gower Street, raining and cold it was too, and went upstairs to the second floor landing. I put my damp raglan over the stairwell banister to let it drip off a bit and then knocked on the kitchen door. Mrs. Pink yelled out for me to come ahead in, which I did, like a lamb to the slaughter, you might say. As soon as I stepped inside, not a word of a lie, I could tell there was trouble on the go. Mrs. Pink was over by the stove stirring a pot of something, her face all red and sweaty from the heat and a look on her would cure the warts for sure.

*Albert*, she cries out, *he's here, Albert!*

And then in he comes, the man himself, charging into the kitchen with his face all screwed up and purple as a beet, foaming at the mouth almost, and shouting as to how I had knocked up his darling little girl and how he was going to have me castrated then and there. He slams his big fist down on the kitchen table and shouts over his shoulder, *Phil! Will!* — and then reaches over and takes me by the shirt front — *I'd see her dead afore she gets mixed up with the likes of you*, he rants on, adding for good measure — *you goddam mick.*

And all the time I could hear the two big bruisers clumping down the back stairs from the third floor.

Was I desperate? Wouldn't you be? All I could think of was how to get free of that crazy crowd. It was clear that darling Violet must be in the family way and had decided to put the blame on me for it, when the Lord knows who had done what with her or where or when, as likely some stray Portuguese sailor off the wharf as anyone else. Well, I wasn't going to be the one to hang for that if I could help it, not even if I was the real culprit.

Anyway, I hauls off and punches Albert Pink right smack in the nose, and that made him blink let me tell you, except he didn't let go of the front of my shirt.

So then I grabs hold of this half full bottle of milk that was there on the kitchen table and lands it down as hard as I could right on the top of that big bald skull and thanks be to God that did the trick, in just the nick of time, too, because he leaves go of my shirt and drops to the floor just as those two brothers of hers comes storming into the room with pure murder on their minds, you can be sure. I didn't wait to wish them good evening, no sir, just grabbed up what I thought was me own cap from the counter, except it wasn't, it was that one that blew off me head back there when we was coming aboard, and flew out the door and down the stairs lickety-split, fast as my legs could take me, faster even, because I must have jumped halfways down the first flight I was that scared. I could hear Mrs. Pink behind me, screaming out at the top of her lungs.

*He's murdered him, Lord Jesus save us, he's after murdering him.*

Phil and Will chased after me down the road a ways, but I had the head start and I was faster afoot than them big fellows anyway. I left them well behind around the Cochrane Hotel, the two of them cursing and swearing and shaking their fists after me, and then ran down along Water Street and down into that laneway back there. There was some old canvas stuff and nets and the like piled up alongside, so I just covered myself over and set down to wait for it to get dark. By and by, I sees the two of you coming across the wharf and I says to myself, 'Lord God, that's Mr. Quigley, for sure!' and sure enough so it was. I figured it would be dark by the time you got back from wherever you was going, so I just squatted down and waited and waited and then, well, here we are, boys, I says, here we are.

## THE PRIEST'S TALE CONCLUDED

There they were, yes indeed, and what to do now, what could they do? How could they get Jerry Boogee off the hot plate without falling into the soup themselves? Would the Royal Newfoundland Constabulary help, perhaps? If they took him along to the station, protect him at least from the avenging brothers? Probably not a good idea, they decided. Albert Pink would have laid a charge by this time and what chance would poor Jerry have, his word against the Pinks'. What to do, what to do?

Now it happened that the *Dromore* was set to sail on Sunday noon, the next day actually, and the more they thought about it, the more it seemed to them that they should try to take Jerry along with them. As First Mate, Uncle Frank Reddy was a senior officer, of course, and senior officers could sometimes bring along a member of the family, free-of-charge or for only a token fee, as long as there was the un-booked space and the master gave his okay for it. Harold Gallant was Captain at that time and he readily consented when Uncle Frank presented Jerry as a cousin from the Codroy Valley. The poor lad was out of work, he told the Captain, a common enough situation in those times, who was trying to get down to see an uncle living in the Boston area who might be able to find him some work there. When he went to fill in the passenger registry, Uncle Frank chewed on his lip for a bit and then wrote in the name 'Jerry Quigley'.

The *Dromore* set sail in the morning, bound for Halifax and American ports. While they were laying up overnight at the India Wharf in Boston, Jerry Boogee disappeared with not a single word of thanks or farewell. He took Dad's papers with him too, and on top of that lifted forty dollars in American bills out of Uncle Frank's dresser drawer. Apart from calling the ingrate a few choice names, there was really nothing they could do. They couldn't contact the Boston police without having to explain to the Captain how Jerry Quigley had suddenly turned into Jerry somebody else, because that would almost certainly mean they'd lose their jobs, and maybe have to face something even worse, like a charge of aiding and abetting a fugitive from justice perhaps. Silence was obviously the only prudent course open to them, and Dad gave Uncle Frank twenty dollars from his own small poke to help even things out a bit.

When they got back to St. John's, they made a few cautious enquiries and found out that there had indeed been a warrant put out for the arrest of one Gerard Bougoise, wanted for assaulting one Albert Pink, Shipping Agent and resident of New Gower Street. And then they read, in that night's *Evening Telegram* that a positive identification had been made of a Church Lads Brigade cap found floating just off the Furness-Withy wharf, a cap with the letters PP sewn on the inside, belonging, without a doubt, to Mr. Pink's son Phil. The cap had been stolen by the aforesaid Bougoise when he fled the scene of the crime. A dispute over wages was behind it all, according to Mr. Pink, with the accused claiming for monies to which he was not entitled.

Fortunately, Mr. Pink had not been seriously injured in the ensuing altercation. The police, meanwhile, had not ruled out the possibility that the fugitive had fallen into the cold harbour waters while being hotly pursued and had probably drowned, although no body had as yet been recovered.

"My dear God," gasped a shocked Uncle Frank Reddy, "They think he went and drowned, Pius. They think he's dead."

Silence, needless to say, was again the best course, for Jerry Bougoise as well as for themselves. "We can thank the Lord, I suppose," Dad said to Uncles Frank, "that you didn't put him down under his own name."

Time passed. They never forgot Jerry, of course, and Dad always had the worry that his papers might turn up tied into a bank robbery or something in the States. But not a word did they ever hear from or about the runaway, which I suppose is not too surprising, keeping in mind that in all of Newfoundland there was hardly a soul to wonder about what might have happened to Jerry Boogee or to be concerned whether he was dead or alive. One or two of the Brothers, perhaps. Perhaps Peter Cleary.

So it's about a dozen years later, with the war and all that in between and over with, a sunny afternoon around the end of June, 1947 or '48. Dad, sadly a widower by this time, is back on Stratton's Road in Corner Brook, sitting at his kitchen table tying up a few salmon flies, when a knock comes on the front door. When he opens up he finds an American serviceman standing on the porch steps, a tall Air Force corporal with sandy close-cropped hair and a long freckled face. Dad can see a jeep parked out on the roadway and the first thing that occurs to him is that the fellow has gotten himself lost.

"Good day to you, sir," says he, "and what can I do for you then, Corporal?"

"Sir," says the Yank, taking off his brevet and tucking it under his left arm, "My name is Wallace, sir, Bob Wallace. Would you be Mr. Pius Quigley, sir?"

He certainly was, says Dad, while the corporal consulted a piece of paper he had in his right hand. And is Dad's brother-in-law Mr. Frank Reddy, one time the First Mate on a ship called the *SS Dromore?* Well, yes, he is, or was, confirmed Dad, wondering, naturally, what in the name of heaven was going on and then waving and ushering his mysterious visitor into the house.

"Sir," says the mysterious Bob Wallace, when they are settled down in the front room, "I was asked to deliver this to you, sir, and to put it straight into your very own hands if I could." And with that, he took a fat manila paper packet out of his jacket and handed it to Dad, who looked at it like it was a live coal but was too surprised not to accept it. The thing is sealed all around with thick black tape of some sort and has 'PIUS QUIGLEY, CORNER BROOK WEST, NEWFOUNDLAND' printed on it in black capitals.

"And what in heaven's name is this, Corporal? Do you know what it is then?"

"Tell the truth, I don't know what's in it, Mr. Quigley. Somebody asked me to deliver this to you and I promised I would and that's all I know about it, God's truth, sir." He got up to leave, then, but of course he wasn't to get off that easy. Dad poured them out a finger or two of scotch whiskey and then cut open the mysterious package with his penknife.

I'm sure you've already guessed what was inside. Dad's ancient seaman's card, his faded and creased birth certificate, risen from the grave as it were, ghostly objects emerging out of the mists of the past. And also fifty, fifty mind you, one-hundred-dollar US bank notes, with a note wrapped neatly around the lot.

*Dear Pius and Frank,*

*I hope you can forgive what I did back in Boston and I sure hope you did not get into any trouble on my account. I should have gone back and faced the music but the truth is I was just too scared. I hope this makes up a bit for what I did. God bless you, Pius, and God bless Frank.*

*Jerry Bennett (Bougoise)*

"Jerry was my best friend," explained Bob Wallace. "We met in basic training and then we served together over in Europe. He was transferred to the Pacific and I got posted back to the States and when we said goodbye he handed me that package and made me swear that if he didn't come back to do it himself ... well, here I am, Mr. Quigley."

"So Jerry won't be, then," says Dad, "coming back, that is."

The other swallowed hard, downed the last of his whiskey and shook his head at the proffered bottle. "I'm real sorry to say he won't be, Mr. Quigley. Died in an accident, Jerry did, in Hawaii. Went and drowned, would you believe it, got himself caught in one of those undertows they have out there. And he couldn't swim a stroke, you know, the damn fool. When I heard about it, well, I pulled every string I could to get up to Ernest Harmon so I could do what he asked me."

"I see," says Dad, "and was he married? Any children?" Again, his visitor shook his head. No wife, no kiddies, no family. So now Jerry Boogee really was drowned, this time for sure, the last of his unfortunate line.

"By the way, Frank Reddy is gone too, Corporal, torpedoed off Iceland in '43. In the Merchant Marine he was, like me. Look here, I can't thank you enough for coming all the way up here, for taking so much trouble over this. But Jerry didn't really owe us anything like this, y'know, nothing like this."

"Oh, I figure you guys must have done something for him, Mr. Quigley. I know he always had something on his mind, something that was always bothering him, like. He was going to come home with me, y'know, Jerry was. Going to work my dad's old place, we were. The old farm."

There was tear glinting in the corporal's eye as they stood and shook hands at the front door. At the bottom of the porch steps he hesitated and turned back and looked at Dad with a puzzled or anxious expression on his face.

"I was just down and had a look, Mr. Quigley."

"At that place where Jerry grew up?"

They could only stare sadly at each other for a few seconds, thinking to themselves of all the bad things Jerry Bennett Bougoise Quigley Boogee must have been carrying around in the curly-topped head of his. Dad patted the younger man on the arm and watched him climb heavily into the jeep and take off down the road. Alone again, he sat and sipped and mused on the strange twists and turns that mark the human condition. The next day he gave Father O'Hara one of the banknotes to say a *tertium* for Jerry's soul. The rest went into the bank, where it sat and waxed until it came time for me to go off to St. FX.

## BOOZEY'S FINALE

Here, you might as well finish this one off too, gentlemen. No, no, nothing for me, thank you. I might have the name for it, but the truth is I never touch the stuff myself. The moniker is from the family name, you see, not from any drinking habits. Truth to tell, my sobriety is the only reason the old man trusts me to run the barroom for him at all.

Now I tell from your faces you're a little skeptical about the tale you just heard, and I can't say I blame you an inch. I can still recall how I felt myself after the Quick had finished it, lighting up a Royal Blend and leaning back to watch him fork my lucky catch into his face, washing it down with gulps of boiled black tea. It was a grand night, too, for considering heavy matters, with the wind softly sighing in the trees, the crackle of our campfire, the purling of the stream off in the dark.

"Well, I must say," I finally said to the priest-to-be, "I must say, that's a tale of luck indeed. Lucky that Jerry whatever-his-name-was had a conscience, and lucky he had a buddy who was remarkably honorable and honest. Lucky too, I suppose, that your dear old Dad survived the war and Jerry didn't. The trouble is, as I see it, is that to call what happened to your Dad 'luck' sort of renders the word meaningless, doesn't it? I mean, we're all lucky just to be born at all, and lucky somebody did this and not that, and lucky we don't get hit by a car or whatever. I mean, I'm lucky I didn't drown today, landing that grilse."

The Quick looked mildly irritated, which made me smile to myself in the dark for having got his goat, and shook his head. He began wearily:

"You are confusing cause-and-effect with luck, Boozy. That money has put me into St. FX and, God willing, will see me into the seminary in the fullness of time. In that, my pagan friend, I see the hand of God at work, the working out of divine will, if you like. Order out of chaos, good out of evil.

No, no, the luck of the matter … I asked you to mark this well, Boozy, but as usual you never seem to see the obvious … the luck, my friend, was back there in '36 or '37. That sudden gust of wind, my friend, the one that lifted the CLB cap off Jerry Boogee's head and sent it flying off into St. John's harbour. There it is, Boozy, that's the stroke of pure unasked-for, un-adulterated luck, the unassisted, unplanned, unhoped-for event that made all that followed so easy to happen, if not inevitable. A great convenience it was, you see, finding that cap, convenient for the constabulary, for the Pinks, for Dad and Uncle Frank, and, of course, for Jerry Boogee, too. The police could close the book on the case, or at least put the matter aside, with everything explained, everything rationalized. The Pinks could pocket Jerry's wages and make up anything they wanted, to cover Violet's sorry situation. And there they were, Dad and Uncle Frank, off the hook, too, of all, if not least, there was Jerry Boogee, free now to become a new man, to be reborn, as it were, down in the United States of America."

"What hogwash," I told him, "the will of his God dependent on a puff of wind." But he only shrugged, shaking his head at my obtuseness, and I let it go at that because we were both yawning and ready for a good night's sleep by this time. I crawled into my sleeping bag and watched through the tent flap as he said his prayers, kneeling alongside the embers of the campfire like one of those Jesuit martyrs. A question popped into my head just as I was ready to drop off and I interrupted his devotions to ask him: "I don't suppose you know what became of it, do you? Violet's baby?"

I don't suppose he'd ever considered the matter. At any rate, all I got was another shrug and then he was back to saying his rosary. *I hope you include it in your prayers*, I felt like saying to him, *and poor old Jerry Boogee as well.* Then I fell asleep, the river weeping to itself out in the night, as if it were carrying along with it all the sins and sorrows of the world.

# SQUEEK ARRIVES

*T*he trouble today is with the *who* of it all. That is, with *who* is to speak, or to be spoken of. Which voice, whose voice. Or tense, too. Time, after all, tense. He stands, stood, by the window, looking out. Or I stand, stood, by the window, looking …

The 'who'. The *who* is myself, of course, Mr. Michael Aloysius Prince, standing by his front parlour window, being looked in on by the World. It is the way of it today he feels, the eye of the World glaring in on him. Standing at, to him, the right hand margin of the scored and much-painted jamb, front thigh of left leg pressed to the sill of the deep well, pinched face just off the centre muntin, a face half, more than half, almost all in fact, blocked from the World's eye by sagging drapery, sham Florentine, faded floral patterns of unnatural symmetry and repetition. Even as he warily watches the World looking in on him, his own pale eye registers sun-drained glories of blue and reseda, nile and salmon.

So I stand to the right hand side of the parlour window, holding ruined drapery panels slightly apart, eyes above but almost level with the long unmoved and now unmovable centre rail, face three quarters, more even, concealed by her faux antique tapestries with their once-brave but now cowed hues. It is one of the fearful days, I do not know why, as if all that is on the outside of the speckled, pitted pane is weighing in against it, a heavy oleaginous tide insisting itself inward. I feel a dry husk myself, desiccated, and crushed I would be, enfolded into the stuff of the world should it break through, should it engulf the transparency between us. Not liquefied or liquidly revived, only swept along as a myriad of gritty particles, specks of matter or whatever, not further soluble, unconnected, disconnected, not even an 'It' anymore, let alone a 'Who'. Alas poor Michael Prince, one might say, rolling an iota of poor Michael-Prince material in its pod of time and space, between thumb and forefinger.

Mister Michael Aloysius Prince, Esq., gentleman-widower, of Number 17 Burkes Road, Town of Corner Brook West, Crown Colony of Newfoundland, stands patiently at his parlour window, waiting. It has snowed overnight; the street is covered, the front garden white and still, the poplars starkly poised with cranky black arms out-thrown as if to protest the scene. Winter is hard enough as it is, he sourly thinks, without piling a springtime like this on top of it, doubly-so if you have more than a smack of age and your fair share of the fleshly shocks to-boot. The sun is on the snow now, too, making it painful to look upon, so he must stand shaded to the side of the window, a ruined eye on the cold, wet world. Should be totally done over to tell the truth, the front window, such a worn out old thing, the pane speckled and dulled with time, fine cracks like wrinkles in the ancient putty. Ratty old curtains, too, faded orange and reseda, damson and rose.

Going to Mass is Mr. Prince, to chew on old bones with the Father and the Son and the Holy Ghost. Recurrent and profound questions to mull over, yet here he stands, his head full of remembering when she had picked them out of the Eaton catalogue, genuine Italianate floral classics, hints of blue and salmon and so on. Rough feel they had to the touch when you pulled them back or shut them against the dark, and overbold, grand for such a modest room.

The grand notions she used to have, the grand ideas.

Any minute now, Arthur Spurrell's jitney will form itself out of the world's white furnace, materialize at the front gate, its dark metallic bulk soiled with road slush and fouled snow, thumping and quivering and putt-putting grey fumes from its backside, a live thing come to ferry me across the brook to St. Henry's. God help the Old Clump on his way to Easter Sunday Mass, on his way to stick up for his just deserts and yes, Squeek would come again, indeed he will, as he has faithfully every Sunday and every Holy Day of Obligation these five years or more. Mr. Arthur 'Squeek' Spurrell, great engenderer, five he has, or perhaps six by now, and a missus of large proportions, all living somehow together in a four-room shack somewhere down towards Curling. While I, Michael A. Prince, because there is no justice at all in this world, nor likely anywhere else, lives all by his lonesome in a two-storey house with four bedrooms, large untended back and side yards and a nice picket fence running around the whole of it. He wants the house, Squeek does. He would put the Old Slindger down in a flash if it would get him the house. And hasn't the Old Piddler hinted, as Squeek has reported to the missus, yes, on more than one occasion hinted, services to be rewarded, recompense for kissing the Old Noddy's behind, running favours at all times, day or night, whatever the weather?

> — And how is your good missus then, Mr.
> Spurrell, with the miserable spring we're
> having?
> — She is suffering through it, Mr. Prince,
> suffering through it like all the rest of us.

And the kids with the colds now, too, would
you believe it, after being so sound all winter.
– Do you give them the cod liver oil, Mr.
Spurrell? They say, you know, if you don't
want the colds, then take your cod liver oil
every day all the winter.
– Oh Lord, Mr. Prince, sure they takes it by
the gallon, gallons we goes through, but they
still comes down with the colds every spring.

She used to take it too, Mr. Doyle's oily nostrum,
and anything else she could get her hands on, liver
pills, syrups and brews of dubious mixture, smearings
of pungent liniments and ointments, till her breath
had the reek of the fish house and her skin was as
mottled as a poxy leaf. She suffered too, and such a
long time it took her to die. He hears her even yet, at
night when he lays awake tracing cracks in the bedroom
ceiling, her shuffle along the upstairs landing, the
twist of the door handle turning. He has taken to
lodging a chair under the handle. What do you think
they would say if they knew that? If Mrs. Breen,
housekeeper spy, told them he was hearing their
mother sighing in the winter night, was barricading
himself against her scuffling, rasping entrance? Have
him in the home, they would, and the house sold,
which was all they wanted anyway.

– How long then, Mr. Spurrell, do you expect
you'll be in Purgatory, eh? Ever think on
that, do you?
– I expects it to be a bloody good rest, Mr.
Prince, a bloody nice holiday, truth to tell.
– Taking into account the Indulgences and so

forth. How do they work, I wonder? Ten days here, a week off there. I mean, if there's no Time, do you see?

— No time at all is just what I got, Mr. Prince. None at all most of the time.

— But there's no Time there, you know. In Eternity. Isn't that what they say?

— Yes, that's the truth, skipper, absolutely. Like I was remarking to the missus just last night, Time depends, I says to her, upon the comparability of one stage or state with another. Do you know what I mean now, Mr. Prince?

— And did she go along with you on that one, Mr. Spurrell?

— Oh we seldom falls out, Mr. Prince, when it comes to things of such nature, seldom if ever. *Yes, Art me dear,* she says right back at me, *sure where there's no change of state there cannot be a comparative duration of Time.* Her exact words, Mr. Prince, true as I'm sitting here. *Cannot be,* she says. *But then,* says she, and she's a great one for the god-stuff, Mr. Prince, as well you know, *a body has to change,* she says, *in the place you're talking about.* Would have to change, y'see, or else nobody could ever get out of it.

— Ah yes, yes. I see. Oh, the real jesuette, Mr. Spurrell, your missus is, the real jesuette.


Mr. Michael Prince, Purgatorial Candidate First Class, does not feel reassured. On the one hand Words, with a capital *W*, on the other, Time, and all of it soon gone — the lot of it, gone soon enough.

Even Eternity must take Time. Squeek Spurrell's tortured eye regards him keenly in the rear view mirror. Undertaker's look, that. Wants the house. House of the *Dead-and-Gone* or *Soon-to-Go*.

> – No Time in Eternity, though. Do you find
> that a comfort, Mr. Spurrell, or not?"
> – Bloody little time here, either. I always hoped
> there was plenty of it there, time to kill almost.
> As they say when you're the dearly departed,
> you'll be resting at so-and-so's parlour, you'll
> be laid to rest and all that. If there's no rest,
> Mr. Prince, then what's the good of it then?
> – No good to it then, is that what you think?
> – Bloody right, if you ask me. Like the missus
> says, Mr. Prince, *if there's no rest there, then*
> *there's no rest at all*, that's for sure. So put
> your feet up while you can, me Old Son,
> that's only thing to do.

I wish the hell he would not stare at me backwards like that. Feeling of a hearse his old cab is getting to have. Sizing me up for the box. He will be hinting after me about the house again when we get back, fixing himself up with a cup of tea like he already owned the place. A desperate man making his desperate way, looking after his own interests. Way of the world, and why not? Get in there, butter up the Old Rumper. By Jesus, had he a signature, he'd be putting the pillow over my face in a flash, I'm sure. Suffering in his own little hell, poor Squeek. Or, like that fellow wrote, there's no one there. No time to be there.

You can't get a sensible word out of the priests either. Not since they got rid of the Redemptorists at any rate;

urbane, scholarly sort of men from the mainland, knew a thing or two about what it was all about. Not like these new fellows, all locals, right from the Codroy Valley or somewhere, with straw still stuck behind their ears and a twang on them would shame a Jew's harp.

"And sure what's the problem now, Mr. Prince? Sure you can be certain the Good Lord will provide all the time needed to save your soul, all the time in the world."

In the world, yes, but then? And while the clichés and platitudes tumble out, the ordained eyes are taking in like a hawk who is coming out of the ten-o'clock Mass. An Old Tomcod, he thinks me, another wrinkle-browed headwagger, cluttering up the clerical head and day with such nonsense. God deliver him from the Questioners.

Home again, home again, jiggedy-jog.

"Have a cup of tea now, Mr. Prince. Damp out there today. Feels it in your bones, you do."

"I wonder if you'd put a spot of the good stuff in it, Mr. Spurrell. Behind the tray there, on the buffet."

He would do just that, says Squeek, and a wee drop for his own brew too. Why hide it from view, though, the good stuff? She wasn't here any more to tsk! tsk! and grimace at him. Of course, she was here all the same. Oh yes. At night, shuttling along the hallway in her wooly slippers, standing there outside the bedroom door while he lay still, listening to his own breath, not frightened exactly, only wondering. Nothing now but bones and hair after three years, would there be?

"Not that I don't trust Mrs. Breen, you understand. But all the same, lead us not and so on, eh, Mr. Spurrell?"

They sent her in to spy every week, to clean up the place as she was supposed to, no matter how many times he told them he could keep things as tidy as a pin all by himself. Anyway, she didn't do a lick as far as he could tell. She knew where the bottle was kept, though, and he could whiff it off her tea when she sat at the kitchen table interrogating him while pretending to be sociable. Spying she was — oh he seems to be doing his pee and the other all right and giving hisself a good scrubbing now and then and shaving off the whiskers every other day, changing his underwear two or three times a week. Reporting to Boston, reporting to Montreal, Wilf and Jenny.

The impulse comes over him, now and then, to sign the place off right away to poor old Squeek and his runny-nosed crew. Could he? You could bet the shyster would be on the long distance to Wilf in a flash, better come home, my son, and see to your dad, looks like he's gone a bit queer, trying to give the house away. Oh, if he could, he would. He has seen Mrs. Squeek at Mass once or twice, two or three of the young ones clinging to her like unruly tentacles. Yes, let the poor fellow have it, the House of Bones, have it right off.

    – What do you think about it, Mr. Spurrell?
      What does the missus think, I wonder?"
    – What Destiny awaits us, eh, beyond the
      darkness of the grave? I put that to her, Mr.
      Prince, just the other night, assuming, mind
      you, the way I put it to her, assuming there's
      any beyond to it at all. A priori, so-to-speak.
    – And her reply?

Look at the trees, will you. Easter Sunday morning can you believe it? Stark-naked, snow heavy on groaning limbs. Like Time heavy on old arms held aloft, like the spread of stiff reluctant fingers along the middle rail — leafless, sapless. And here he is at last. Good Man Squeek. Good Faithful Squeek. Give it to him I will, straight outright; let shylock Wilf whistle for his interest, Jenny too if she wants to. Shorten my days that would, in that place of Last Time, hasten me into that place where there are no days. No hours, no months or weeks, no years, no tics or tocs, no Time at all. Only words. Full of words it would be, like in the Beginning, Words without Time.

Tom Finn was born and raised in the town of Corner Brook, Newfoundland. After working in New Brunswick, Prince Edward Island and California, he took up residence in Ottawa, A retired federal public servant, Tom has always taken a keen interest in the affairs of his island homeland. He is especially interested in the transformation of the former British colony following the American 'invasion' in the 1940s, and the union with Canada in 1949.